THE SPY THAT WASN'T

And other stories of high achievement

THE SPY THAT WASN'T

And other stories of high achievement

BY
COLIN HESTON

READ-ME.ORG INC.
PUBLISHERS
Australia, New York & Philadelphia

Library of Congress Control Number: 2023940805

ISBN:978-0-911577-69-3 (Paperback)
ISBN: 978-0-911577-71-6 (Digital)

TABLE OF CONTENTS

.

1. A ROMAN HOLIDAY

In 1966 the United Nations Social Defense Research Institute (UNSDRI) was established to conduct research into the international aspects of crime and criminal justice. It was the brainchild of Aldo Moro, on-again-off-again Prime Minister of Italy. Moro, former law professor at the University of Rome, was the unstoppable head of the Christian Democratic Party, full of confidence, grand master of the endless subterfuges within which decisions were made, and where money, especially money, was acquired and distributed.

The institute was located in Rome, on the beautiful Via Giulia, in a medieval building that was once a prison, and directly opposite one of the ancillary buildings of the Italian Ministry of Justice. With much fanfare, Moro managed to allocate 500 million lire startup money to pay for the UNSDRI director general, a large man of African descent from Somalia or maybe the Congo, and a fledgling staff, all Italian of course, of three secretaries, one administrator, and several doormen and couriers. Moro pointed out to the UN directorate in New York, that Italy was donating the entire building as office space, and expected that other nations of the UN would contribute their fair share. The matter was urgent, especially for travel money, an essential food for all UN officials, without which they withered away at their desks. And the defense of societies against crime and insurrection was surely the utmost role for the United Nations, especially for developing countries where

1

insurrection and terror had become the rule, when even the
Director General of the United Nations, Dag Hammarskjöld
was assassinated as he tried to engineer peace in the Congo in
1961. Italy, a former colonial power would do its part.

The institute was located in Rome, on the beautiful Via
Giulia. The office was always busy. The Director General Sup-
reme of UNSDRI had many diplomatic missions to attend to,
endless meetings with important figures of Italy's foreign
ministry, and frequent visits to the Commissary at its sister
U.N. Organization in Rome. the FAO (Food and Agricultural
Organization), located in a massive building, one of
Mussolini's monstrosities, built to administer Italy's colonies.

In 1969, the arrival at UNSDRI of an English speaking
intern from Cambridge England was expected any day, a newly
minted Ph.D. from the Cambridge University's renowned
criminology program. He would head up the Institute's first
research study, funded copiously by the Ford Foundation, to
collect international crime statistics from around the world,
collate the findings, and recommend to the United Nations
General Assembly ways to combat world crime. As the
Americans repeated many times over, there was no sense
developing policies, local or worldwide, if they were not
informed by data. Data, data, data, that was the rant. That said,
it was an Englishman who was expected to take charge, for the
Italians could not quite bring themselves to acknowledge the
superior empirical research capabilities of the Americans.

Professor Franco Ferrapotti, renowned psychiatrist at the
University of Rome, and Procuratore Ugo Di Napolitano,
Supreme Court Magistrate, were seconded from their important positions to supervise the research, approve of its design,
and ensure that the results were accurate and infallible. It was
their signatures that were on the lucrative contract signed with
the Ford Foundation. Ferrapotti, an ebullient, rotund Roman,
balding, a veritable look-alike of Mussolini, saw himself as the

true director of the project, indeed of the whole institute. His partner, Judge Di Napolitano, was a man of Naples as his name implied, a tall, upright gentleman, spoke in a high-pitched, loud voice, a voice rather like that of the Godfather in the movie of that name, only louder, one that penetrated every crack in the old building. His English was heavily accented, drawing out the wonderful vowel sounds of southern Italy, speaking in long legal clauses, as though pronouncing even the punctuation. In contrast, his colleague Ferrapotti, spoke English with a distinct American accent, smooth, monotone, rambling, like a car running idle.

The great halls of the institute were therefore full of the echoes of these two directors, constantly arguing (or seemingly so) with each other. Ferrapotti, having served as a visiting distinguished professor in various American Universities, pointed out that there was no American in the institute and that, if the project were to be conducted successfully, its results accepted by the world scientific community, it would have to be carried out by an American. Di Napolitano demurred, somewhat, though he thought that there was no problem that could not be solved by clear, rational, logical thinking. The "facts" he treated as data (if he must use that ugly word) to be used and interpreted as needed by the policymaker. And since it was the policymaker who interpreted the data, there was no real necessity to demonstrate that the data were "valid" or "accurate" or whatever the social scientists said made their findings "facts." In contrast, Ferrapotti, thought of "facts" as something that he found out when he examined a patient (he had many referred to him from the Vatican), got answers from his probing questions, formed hypotheses about the patient's problem and prescribed the treatment forthwith. Without these "facts" concerning his individual patient, he obviously could not make the appropriate diagnosis, and thus prescribe the correct treatment. It was, for him, as it was for the great father of psychiatry, Sigmund Freud still dominant in the 1960s though slowly being undermined by young radical psychiatrists, a great leap from the analysis of individual cases, to diagnose crime on a mass scale as the project envisaged, dare to prescribe steps to solve the problem of crime at the world level.

Thus, the compromise was to appoint an Englishman.

And now our story begins.

As Di Napolitano and Ferrapotti mounted the few big steps to the Institute, at Via Giulia 52, arguing incessantly, Ferrapotti felt a tug on his leather jacket. The guard on duty stepped out from his glass-enclosed post, pushed past Ferrapotti and grabbed a scruffy looking young man, dressed in shorts, the sign of either an American or Australian, shirt hanging loose, leather sandals, like those worn by many of the neophyte students of the Vatican.

"Halt!" shouted the guard, "non entrare qui!"

The scruffy young man grinned and stepped back. "Doctor Ferrapotti!" he cried.

Ferrapotti stopped in mid-sentence and turned to face this person who spoke English in an accent he had heard only once before, of an Australian he had met in one of his classes when he was a visiting professor at America's prestigious University of Pennsylvania.

"Doctor Ferrapotti! Remember me? I was in your class…"

Ferrapotti looked this scraggly fellow up and down. Short in stature, thin, nothing of him. "Oh.. Er..ah..You need a good meal of Italian pasta," said Ferrapotti with a grin. "What can I do for you?"

Di Napolitano looked annoyed. It was beyond his comprehension that Ferrapotti, or any Italian for that matter, would bother to acknowledge any foreigner, especially an English speaking one, who came up to him in the street. Besides, it was a security risk. But this did not deter Ferrapotti. He looked for every moment to be flattered. To be recognized by a former student or anyone else for that matter, he welcomed.

The Aussie looked up, pushed the guard's hand away from his arm. "This is an amazing coincidence," he said, "I'm here for a two-day stopover on my way home to Melbourne. I thought you were at the University of Rome."

Ferrapotti looked at him, and without any hesitation asked, "oh.. Er..ah..do you want a job?"

"I, I…" stuttered the Aussie, taken aback.

Di Napolitano turned away and sprinted up the steps leading to the Institute, calling back over his shoulder, "basta, Franco. Non fai niente stupido!"

Ferrapotti grinned at the Aussie. "Oh.. Ah.. Don't mind him," he said, "he's a judge so he's used to giving orders."

"I, I don't know what to say."

"Yes or no? Oh.. Er.. It's a great opportunity to work for the United Nations. On the frontier of international criminology," urged Ferrapotti.

"But I, I'm on my way back to Australia. I have a research assistant position lined up there…"

"Ah.. Er.. Come on!" Ferrapotti grabbed him roughly by the arm. "Come see your new office! Beautifully frescoed ceilings. Just like the Vatican library!"

The Aussie allowed himself to be pulled up the steps and past the *pezzi grossi,* the several doormen and couriers, through the double doors, the well-armed guard staring at his log book, trying not to notice, dialing a number on the intercom. The long corridor, expansive and frescoed from top to bottom appeared before them. The sounds of Di Napolitano's lilting voice echoed from his office at the far end. Ferrapotti's office was right next to his.

Overwhelmed and confused, the Aussie struggled along, his knees weak, his eyes of course taking in the wonders of Italian faux Renaissance frescoes. They were half way down the corridor when a door opened, a very large glass door, revealing the biggest of all offices, two secretaries typing away at their Olivettis, one each side of the massive carved door to the Director General's office. Ferrapotti dragged the Aussie in.

"Is the Supreme General in?" he asked, looking at one of the secretaries then to the other. None looked up. One, or possibly both, murmured, "he's in, but does not want to be disturbed. Very important business coming in from the UN Secretariat in New York."

Ferrapotti of course ignored the response and barged right in, pulling his Aussie charge with him.

"Er, ah, Professor, Doctor Supreme Secretary General, I want you to meet our project director for our new Ford Foundation grant, er…"

The director general of the Institute lounged back in his heavily padded office chair, beautifully crafted with leopard skin, taken from a leopard that he himself had shot on his recent trip back home in Somalia, or maybe the Congo.

"Ah, yes. The Ford foundation. Pity it was not the Mercedes Foundation. But I suppose, beggars can't be choosers," said the general in his very deep voice, and a big smile, one that was required of all African UN Staff members. And what is this you have brought me?" He looked at the small, overly tanned young white male, his hair too long and poorly combed.

Ferrapotti grinned and replied, "Ah.. Oh.. This is er…"

"Dennis Cotter," put in the Aussie. "My name is Dennis Cotter and I'm from Melbourne Australia."

"Yes, that's right. Dennis. One of my very successful students from the greatest school of America the Wharton School of the University of Pennsylvania, where I taught on their request the history of criminology, which of course you know, is one of Italy's main claims to academic excellence. We pioneered the science of criminology, Lombroso and others,…"

"Yes, yes," said the general, fingering his many medals impatiently. "But if you will pardon me, I must leave on an urgent mission. There is a meeting in Strasbourg…"

"Strasbourg? But that's where the Council of Europe meets, isn't it?" asked Ferrapotti.

"Yes, that's right. I have offered our services to the COE."

"Oh well done! And congratulations!" said Ferrapotti, knowing full well that if Di Napolitano found out, he would raise hell.

The director general left, carrying his diplomatic pouch, walking cane, and a set of car keys, with a very large key ring made of ivory, the Mercedes logo carved into it. Ferrapotti looked at Dennis, and said in his usual blunt way, "ah.. Er.. oh.. don't mind him. We need him as our face to the UN, an organization that takes seriously only those from developing countries. We allow them to occupy all top administrative positions because we know we can easily bribe them into doing whatever we want. Did you notice his key ring? The first thing he did when the foreign minister announced his appointment as director of the institute, was to go out and buy a black Mercedes."

Dennis was taken aback, and should have taken this rant as a warning. But the fact was he saw only the promise of being paid while he indulged in a year or so in Rome, the most beautiful place on earth. It was an opportunity that he could not pass up, no matter how crazy and surreal it seemed. To be offered a job, by a world renowned professor who could not remember his name, to work in a beautifully frescoed medieval building. What more could one ask for? So, without even asking how much the job paid, he instead asked, "so what is the project I will be working on?"

Ferrapotti appeared not to hear the question. "Oh.. Ah.. Come along," he said. "I'll introduce you to my good friend and illustrious judge, Di Napolitano. We call him the

Consigliere. Without him, this Institute could not function."

Di Napolitano stood up from his desk and walked around to shake Dennis's hand. "Very pleased to meet you," he said, his voice always loud, no matter where or with whom. "If you are recommended by Dr. Ferrapotti, I know you must be outstanding!"

Dennis managed to release his hand from Di Napolitano's iron grip, and replied, "well thank you sir, but I don't know, I haven't really…"

Ferrapotti looked Dennis in the eye. It was his psychiatrist's look, one meant to penetrate the facial veneer of his subjects, to make them think that he was looking right inside their mind. "Oh.. Er.. Young man," he said, "this is an opportunity that will never come again. It will make you famous. It will be the very first study of world crime. And conducted under the auspices of the United Nations, and more important, with the scholarly imprint of the great legacy of Italian Criminology, where criminology was first established as a science."

Dennis felt the small slap of Ferrapotti's hand on his shoulder. How could he refuse? "OK. I'll do it. But I need a few details."

"No problem! Just step in here and I will introduce you to our administrative director and she will take care of all your immediate needs."

Ferrapotti stepped away and hurried to Di Napolitano's office, just as a glass door opened and there stood a dark headed young lady, dressed in what appeared to be a kind of female designer simulation of a Carabiniere uniform, with a red stripe running down the side of tight pants, and black jacket, stretched across the fulsome chest, collar and cuffs braided with silver, everything edged in scarlet. Her skin was the pale white of a Northerner, her jet black hair, though, flowing in careful waves over her shoulders. All this and more Dennis took in with a gulp of air.

"I am Andrea. Come, please take a seat by my desk and we will get your details," she said in broken English, though very business-like.

Dennis was, understandably, most confused and not a little concerned. He had a plane to catch the next morning back to Melbourne. He had nowhere to stay beyond this one night. He had no money to extend his stay at the *pensione* he had found just around the corner from Campo dei Fiori.

"Well, I don't know. I mean, I was only walking by. It was pure chance I ran into Doctor Ferrapotti. And I don't really know what he wants me to work on."

"Oh, don't worry!" said Andrea with a big sigh. "È il modo in Italiano, sai? You'll get used to it."

"Modo what?"

"Oh, sorry. It's the Italian way, especially in Rome. Take every day as it comes. Lo sai?"

"OK. Maybe easy for you. But what will I do about my plane ticket? And where will I stay if I take on the job? I mean, there's so much to do. And my family are expecting me to arrive home day after tomorrow."

Andrea just smiled and began writing on a form. "So, your full name, please?"

"What for?" asked Dennis, defensively.

Andrea looked at him impatiently. "Now, let's get this done so I can help you find a place to stay and take care of your plane ticket. Hopefully you are on Alitalia?

"Yes, I am."

"Then there's no problem. We will get you a refund. Now, your name?"

And so it went. Andrea filled out what she called a "Special Service Agreement" with the United Nations. When she came to the amount that he would be paid, Andrea frowned. "Did they tell you how much you would be paid?"

"No. But I haven't really agreed to do his yet, have I?"

"Once you sign this form you have. You should ask them for more money. This is not enough to live on," Andrea said.

"Seriously?"

"Yes. Seriously."

***

Dennis found an "apartment" right beside Piazza Navona. an incredible find, for just 10,000 lire a month. It consisted of a small space under a stairwell with room for a bed and a toilet, a hand basin and an electrical outlet with a small table on which there sat an electric kettle. The apartment had been described as "fully furnished," which technically Dennis supposed was accurate. Never mind, Dennis imagined himself a top researcher living in splendor in Rome, the most beautiful city in the world. Lygon street near Melbourne University where his research assistant position awaited him, could hardly compete.

The trouble was, though, he had no idea what he was supposed to be doing in his new prestigious job, except that, since the The Englishman from Cambridge had not arrived, he had been called into Ferrapotti's office and told that he was to be the sole director of the project and given an extra 40,000 lire a month to make up for the added responsibility. Dennis tried to ask in a roundabout way what he was supposed to be doing, what the project was all about, but had received no information from Ferrapotti, who was constantly talking through the wall to his colleague Di Napolitano, laughing and joking in Italian, dictating letters to his (everyone's) secretary, Andrea who continued to wear her Carabiniere uniform look-alike. But never mind, it was enough for Dennis to walk to his office each day, down the glorious Via Giulia, stopping at a crowded bar for a cornetto and morning cappuccino, peering in the windows of plush shops that displayed costly antiques or fine clothing.

After several weeks he discovered the institute's library, hidden away on the second floor looking out over the Via Giulia, inhabited by a librarian and her assistant. No one had thought to mention this to him, though he was a little embarrassed that he had not thought to ask whether the institute had a library. Of course, being the United Nations, as Dennis was to find out much later, all institutes and branches of the U.N. had a library, crammed full mainly of records and reports of the countless meetings it routinely conducted. The librarian was a middle aged Iranian, and her assistant, a tiny shy whisk of a person, who spent her days repairing reports that had been torn, writing in catalog numbers, and rearranging the book shelves. Though she appeared insignificant, almost like a piece of furniture, her darting eyes seemed constantly to take in all that was going on in the library, and at coffee break, she took her espresso with a small group of well-dressed middle aged Italian men in the corner of the small bar that stood conveniently across the street from the Institute. It was rumored (that is, the librarian told Dennis in the manner of a warning) that she was the daughter of the famed Italian politician Giulio Andreotti.

***

Another month went by, and still Dennis had no idea what he was to do, had been given no instructions by Ferrapotti. So at last, one morning, Dennis, tired of doing nothing, something that he could not believe would worry him, since doing nothing in Rome and getting paid for it seemed like such a great idea, he marched into Di Napolitano's office determined to find out what his project was all about and what he must do. He wanted to work, damn it! After his few months in Rome, Dennis should have known better than to do this foolish thing. Indeed, he had consulted Andrea as to whether this was a good idea, and she had warned him against it.

Di Napolitano did not look up, but continued with his

eyes closed, dictating a letter to his secretary, Andrea (everyone's secretary), in careful grammatically correct English. Dennis coughed a little and advanced to the edge of Di Napolitano's desk. Andrea tried to help by asking her boss to repeat a word. This annoyed him as it always did, to be interrupted, even though he was himself the world's worst interrupter. He assumed, as he was a judge of very high standing, that all must stop when he spoke and he must never be interrupted. But Andrea's question caused him to open his eyes and it was then that he saw standing in front of his desk the scruffy Aussie, dressed in his usual open neck shirt, and worst of all, again something Dennis had been warned about by Andrea, Aussie shorts.

"What is this?" barked Di Napolitano. "Mr. Cotter, you are not dressed. Please do so before you enter my office, in fact, before you enter this institute." He closed his eyes again and continued to dictate to Andrea who looked down, trying very hard to hold back a laugh.

Dennis about-turned as though he were a soldier and hurried out of the office and the building, then to Campo Dei Fiori where he would try to find a pair of cheap long pants that fitted him.

***

Dennis could hardly be blamed for concluding that the fiasco of his attempt to consult with Di Napolitano had at last brought about action. The very next morning, Ferrapotti summoned him to his office, all very business-like.

"Er, ah, Dennis. Good. Come. Sit. We are going to Strasbourg tomorrow to begin the project."

"Tomorrow? But Dr. Ferrapotti, I don't know what the project is about, so I haven't done anything on its design." He squirmed uncomfortably in his seat. He received no direct answer. Instead, Ferrapotti called for Andrea. Dennis timidly asked, "why Strasbourg?"

"Er, ah, yes. Of course, you wouldn't know anything about the Council of Europe, coming from where you come."

Dennis guessed that Ferrapotti was telling him that because he was not a European, he is uninformed, probably ignorant. He simply looked blankly back at Ferrapotti and waited.

"In a first for the United Nations, we are combining our project with the Council of Europe. Ford Foundation has given us its permission, in fact they are very pleased. This will be a pioneering project. A world first!" announced Ferrapotti grandly.

Dennis, now agitated and losing his cool, asked belligerently, in typical Aussie style, "and what exactly is this project that I am supposed to be directing, all about?"

Ferrapotti grinned, looked at Andrea then to Dennis. "Oh, ah, er, I thought you knew, you're the director of the project after all."

"But Dr. Ferrapotti, I have tried to ask you what the project is about, even to see the proposal that you sent to the Ford Foundation…"

"Ah, er. oh, that's nothing. But if you want to look at it you can. Andrea make him a copy will you? But I tell you, it's only a very rough outline of what we will really do."

Dennis looked at Andrea, who excused herself so she could go to the library and retrieve a copy of the proposal. He went to follow her out, but Ferrapotti called him back. "She will get it. Come, er ah, sit."

Dennis sat.

"Oh.. Er.. The United Nations works very slowly," said Ferrapotti, gently, or at least for him it was so. "The way we do research in the UN is to have meetings and then we meet again to discuss the reports of those meetings. And then, it will be your job to carry out the recommendations in those reports."

"But who designs the project?" asked Dennis with a frown.

"Oh.. Those at the meetings do. That way we can be sure that everyone is on board and nobody's concerns are ignored."

"So I don't have to do a research design?" asked Dennis, almost relieved, but very worried.

"Not exactly. That's just what they teach you at University. In the real world, especially the complex world of the UN, it's not the way it works," prattled Ferrapotti.

"I think I'd better go to the library and read some reports," mumbled Dennis.

"Ah.. Er.. Oh.. By all means," answered Ferrapotti, amused. "And ask Andrea to come to my office so we can arrange the plane tickets and per diem for each of us. Strasbourg is an expensive place."

***

The combined UN-Council of Europe meeting occurred as scheduled. A total of twelve "experts" as they were all called, plus supportive staff to warm the seats for the experts, take notes, and pass to them special handwritten notes conveyed to them from the Rapporteur, assembled in the cavernous Council of Europe Debating Chamber. Dr. Ferrapotti, Andrea and Dennis attended and sat to one side, though during the entire meeting Dr. Ferrapotti rarely sat, but constantly paraded about the hall, stopping and chatting with whoever was in his path, a look on his face as though he were indulged in some great conspiracy, a smirk of superiority, his eyes dancing around as if to scan the great hall for hidden spies. On the other side were various representatives of the Council of Europe, though it turned out that the only country sending its representatives was the Netherlands, and there was one country represented by an "observer," a representative who sat at the far back of the hall, a very large suitcase sitting in the aisle beside him. This man with a ruddy complexion, lined face and very red cheeks, head shaved, was the observer from East Germany, who, as it turned out, spoke only Russian. He had, however, been invited to observe at the special request of Dr. Ferrapotti, as a sign of good will.

The Rapporteur called the meeting to order and made a special plea that all participants come down from their seats perched way back from the dais, so that all could hear each other speak, and besides as an act of international friendship. Without thinking, Dennis, an obedient person who wanted to please everyone, got up and moved and, surprisingly, others did as well, mumbling and joking as they did so. The Rapporteur, Professor of Law from the esteemed Sorbonne, a veritable Napoleon look-alike, addressed the members in English, with a sonorous French accent that seemed to issue from his large nose:

"Good morning," he tapped the microphone, "I regret the lack of simultaneous translation, but with our small numbers, we did not qualify. Esteemed members, experts and observers. I am honored to serve as rapporteur for this important meeting in which we will develop the necessary protocols for the collection of crime statistics worldwide and will, we very much hope, result in the construction of not only a World Crime Index, but establish a framework for universal transparency in criminal justice. This is a pioneering study, a giant first in collaboration between the Council of Europe and the United Nations."

The delegates and experts all clapped lightly in response to these uplifting remarks. The Rapporteur smiled and raised his hands as if to accept the applause. Dennis was spellbound. He was probably the only person present whose native language was English. How privileged he was! He looked around the chamber and could hardly believe that he was here, among such illustrious people, and most amazing of all, he was going to direct the first ever study of world crime statistics. He was himself clapping. He could not remember having ever before clapped in a meeting of any kind, when he felt a touch to his arm. He turned and looked up to see Dr. Ferrapotti staring down at him, his usual big grin. Ferrapotti leaned over and with his hand cupped over his mouth, whispered loudly, "Oh, ah, this guy is trying to get the Turks into the Council of Europe and the EU. He's a lawyer and they are writing a new criminal code that excludes the death penalty. You know, it's a requirement of the EU that all member states abolish the death penalty. Keep this under your hat."

Before Dennis could answer, though he had nothing to say except some kind of in-awe grunt perhaps, Dr. Ferrapotti had gone to some other delegate to pass on another piece of top secret information. The Rapporteur continued:

"And with those short introductory remarks, I now welcome you all to the Council of Europe and ask that you briefly stand and introduce yourselves." The Rapporteur did not call on anyone to start, because as a skilled Rapporteur he did not want to give any impression of who he thought of first. All must be treated equally here in this illustrious place.

A quintessential European, silver haired, tall and straight, arose and announced, "I am Professor Dr. Der Groot, University of Amsterdam, and Director of Research, Supreme Court of Netherlands."

The mysterious man who had remained at back, stood and said, in broken English, "I observer East Germany, not tell department." He sat down with a bang and then noisily opened his suitcase, retrieved a bottle of vodka and small glass, which he filled, gulped down, and cried "За встречу" (to our meeting!).

Dennis waited for other delegates from other countries to announce their presence. None came forward. His boss, that was how he had come to think of him, Ferrapotti made no attempt to announce himself because he was too busy talking to the Rapporteur, his hand cupped over his mouth almost touching the Rapporteur's ear. Dennis rose slowly. "I am Dennis Cotter, and will be leading the project for Professor

Dr. Ferrapotti and Professor Dr. Di Napolitano, for the United Nations Social Defense Research Institute." All stared at this scruffy individual, dressed in cheap pants and open neck shirt, no tie. His accent, the words rolling inaudibly from his mouth to his chin, revealed his obvious nationality. The East German, greatly excited, immediately reached into his suitcase and pulled out a bottle of beer. "You want?" he called with a big grin.

"Thank you Mr. Cotter," said the Rapporteur with a forced smile. "And are you able to tell us anything of your preliminary design for the project?"

Dennis, deeply embarrassed, had started to sit, nervously stood again. "Like what?" he asked with a touch of belligerence.

The Rapporteur looked away and directed his gaze at the man from Holland, who quickly stood and responded.

"It is our considered opinion that we should start by collecting information only on the numbers of persons in prison throughout the world. This would be phase one. After that, we should then collect information on the crimes that have been committed in every country."

"Oh, er, ah," interrupted Ferrapotti, having taken his seat in the front row, "it should be the other way around. First we count the crimes, then count the prisoners."

Dennis raised his hand and, seeing that the Rapporteur was not looking his way, he stood and coughed loudly. "In America we count crimes by number of crimes reported to the police. It is the most valid, front line measure, unsullied by the complexities of the criminal justice system."

"You are not Australian?" asked the Rapporteur rudely.

"No, I mean I am an Aussie, but I graduated from the renowned criminology program at University of Pennsylvania."

"That explains it," announced Der Groot, full of his cultured superiority. "You are not a lawyer, so you know nothing of the definition of crimes or for that matter criminality."

Dennis sat back in the padded seat, thoroughly embarrassed, and very angry. "What a pompous asshole," he mumbled
to himself. His boss came to the rescue.

"Oh, er, ah, as a psychiatrist I can support Dr. Cotter's
observation. One does not have to be a lawyer to know what a
crime is."

"Mr. Cotter is a psychiatrist?" asked Der Groot imper-
iously.

Dennis, motivated by his boss's support rose quickly and
raised his hand. The Rapporteur pretended not to see him and
looked back to Ferrapotti. But Dennis was not to be dismissed
so easily. "I am a sociologist," he said proudly, "and we know
much more about the entire criminal justice process, the
behavior of police who collect the initial information of crimes
and who have a well-established procedure for recording and
counting them. You have to look at the whole process from
the initial report of a crime through to the end result, the
punishment, depending on the seriousness of the offence, the
final prison term served by the offender."

"Yes, of course," ceded Der Groot, "but what you have
described would require a lifetime of research and is simply not
practical, to collect information of the entire criminal justice
system of every country in the world. Besides, many may not
even have a criminal justice system as you Americans seem to
assume."

"I am not an American," snarled Dennis again, deeply
offended.

The Rapporteur abruptly stood up. "I see that our
morning break is upon us. We shall retire for a tea or coffee as
you prefer, and return in half an hour."

As they made their way up the steps to the exit of the great
debating chamber, Dennis tried very hard to catch up with his
boss. But Ferrapotti was already busily talking in very loud

whispers to the Rapporteur, then to the Dutchman, ignoring the East German, who in any case, remained in his seat with his suitcase, and beckoned wildly to Dennis as he passed, to join him. But Dennis hurried outside, eager to get away from these most obnoxious Europeans, all of them seemingly ignorant of the simple basics of crime statistics. He walked towards the barred and flagged entrance to the Council of Europe compound, when he realized that he should have gone to the toilet. He did not want to return to the chamber, for fear he would meet one of the delegates and would say something he would regret. He looked around for a convenient place. Hardly a tree in sight, but plenty of green grass, and no significant buildings behind which one could hide. Maybe if he simply stood between a couple of the flags, facing away from the building, no one would notice. But of course someone would. He had a feeling of being spied on all the time. And there's nothing worse than that feeling when one wants to pee.

Eventually, Dennis found a bathroom in another part of the building and was able to return to the chamber, ready for the next round. His boss caught up with him just as he was entering the chamber, nudged his elbow, whispered in his ear, his lips almost touching. "Oh, er, ah," he whispered, "keep going. It doesn't matter what they say. We will do what we want. We have the money, they don't." He hurried off to accost some other member, probably Der Groot.

All were assembled, but as yet the Rapporteur had not arrived. Dennis looked around, caught Ferrapotti's sly glance, and maybe a nod towards the door at bottom of the chamber. And there, he saw Andrea emerge, her cheeks rosy, her hand touching her hair as though it were blowing in the wind. In a few moments, the Rapporteur tried impossibly, given his Napoleonic stature, to walk as upright as Charles de Gaulle, his pin striped suit fitting so snuggly that it accentuated his protruding belly, a great match for Andrea's simulated Carabinieri attire.

"Now esteemed delegates," announced the Rapporteur, "we appear to have something of an agreement, or should one say a compromise. Statistics on those convicted of crimes will first be collected. This takes into account the legal definition of when a crime is a crime, which is defined by a conviction. There can be no doubt about that. At the same time, our sociologists will collect information of the number of offenders in prison."

Dennis could not help himself. "After trial or before trial?" he asked.

His boss looked back and frowned. He should shut up. That was the message. The Rapporteur also scowled and shuffled some papers.

"Yes, we know that France has the highest rate of incarceration awaiting trial of any modern country," noted Der Groot with a touch of glee.

"Though an important measure that statistic is not available from French authorities. Besides, this assertion is based on rumor, not fact, and cannot be accepted as true without the relevant data," answered the Rapporteur, looking over his glasses at the rest of the audience, avoiding Der Groot's pompous stare.

The Rapporteur looked at his watch. "It is time for our lunch break. It will be served in the Council of Europe dining room for delegates. Follow our event coordinator, the beautiful Andrea, and she will show you the way. I am told there will be five courses, as there should be, with the best quality French wines. We will reconvene in three hours."

Immediately all rose and made their ways to Andrea. The East German had understood well enough and was already by her side, grinning and licking his lips.

The afternoon session was cancelled for reasons unknown, though Ferrapotti had whispered to Dennis that all was well, and that a solution to the difficulties would be reached by the next morning. He, Der Groot and the Rapporteur would meet for dinner. Dennis was not invited. It was a chance for him to get to know Andrea, Ferrapotti had said with a wink.

RESOLUTION

"I am pleased to open this, our second session, of the United Nations and Council of Europe collaboration to address the problem of world crime," announced the Rapporteur with greatly affected pride. "After conversations delegates had at dinner and afterwards, there is a draft of our resolutions now available from our most beautiful administrative assistant. Mademoiselle Andrea will now read out the draft of our deliberations."

Andrea, now dressed in a sleek two piece suit, the top a snug fit and the bottom styled as a miniskirt, always the colors of the Carabinieri, stepped up to the podium that had been specially erected for her. Dennis was spellbound, both by her amazing composure and by the shock he felt that these people had already drafted a report of deliberations, even though the major aspects of the project had never been addressed. He could—almost—accept that he was not included in the out-of-meeting deliberations, given his apparent very junior position as accidental director of the research, nevertheless, he had to gulp very hard to swallow the inferior position into which he had been relegated. So far, he could see no reason why he was even dragged along to this meeting.

Andrea began:

"*Considering*, that in light of increases in crime worldwide, the World Crime Project will collect crime data from all member countries of the United Nations and the Council of Europe, and...

"*Acknowledging* the implications world crime has for world order, the project will be carried out in a timely, if not urgent, manner to address the many concerns of world crime for citizens.

"*Observing,* that the rise in world crime will place a burden on the capacity of prisons of most if not all member nations, particular attention will be given to the numbers of inmates currently residing in prisons.

"*Understanding,* that the definition of crime varies according to the different procedures and laws of each member country, data will be collected concerning only the general categories of crime such as homicide, assault and theft.

"*Accepting* the fact that crime also varies according to economic conditions, data will be collected concerning the social status of the offenders, whether rich or poor, the particular measures of these categories to be left to the appropriate technical experts.

"*Realizing* the importance of this research for the economic and social progress of developing nations, the Director of Research will give special attention to developing countries, their social and cultural problems and differences concerning crime and criminal justice.

"*Recognizing* that for many member nations, crime and justice are politically sensitive problems, the project results will not be published in any public forum, without the permission of every member nation.

"*Accepting* furthermore, that this research is highly technical as well as sensitive politically, significant research design decisions must be approved by every participating member nation, before the project can continue forward.

"*Approving* the general design of this important project will be contingent on the director of the research project presenting a research design and preliminary report to this body one year from now."

Andrea looked up at her audience, collected her papers, and stepped away as light applause followed her to her seat.

The Rapporteur from his supervising chair stood and clapped excessively.

Dennis, however, had shrunk back into his padded seat, angry as he had never been before, or at least since he was a three year old. His immediate impulse was to call them a bunch of nincompoops. In fact, he raised his hand, waved it actually, but the Rapporteur's eyes had already landed on Der Groot, who responded accordingly.

"May I congratulate you, Monsieur Rapporteur and your very hard workers, for having drafted an excellent report of our important deliberations." He turned to look at Dennis. "And Mr. Cotter, I congratulate you on your position as project director and urge you to undertake the recommendations of our meeting as soon as you are able. Mademoiselle Andrea has provided an excellent blueprint for going forward. I commend her and thank you all for your insightful contributions."

Dennis forced a smile, the corners of his mouth quivering with pent up anger. He spied his boss Ferrapotti, grinning gleefully, as he did the rounds of all participants, whispering loudly in their ears. Then, without quite realizing it, he found himself standing in his place, his hand up as though asking to go to the bathroom. "Monsieur Rapporteur!" he called.

"The chair recognizes Mr. Cotter of UNSDRI."

"What about race? Why is that not included as a variable?"

Immediately he had said it, he knew he was in trouble. It was the way he said it. He should have said simply, "Do you think race should be included along with the other social factors you recommend?"

For once, Ferrapotti stopped his whispering and his persistent grin faded. The Rapporteur's jaw dropped, and Der Groot, now also angry, rose from his seat. He looked across the cavernous chamber, no more than a dozen people scattered around the front rows, a chamber built to seat several hundred,

his lips dripping with pomposity, his countenance so patron-
izing, and informed Dennis of his utterly ignorant mistake:

"I cannot speak for the rest of Europe, but The Netherlands certainly does not collect crime or any other type of social
data according to race. That would be a policy of outright
racism. It is racial profiling, as your American government even
calls it. It is time that the United States learned from Europe
how to include its ethnics into its supposed diverse democracy."

Dennis went very red, his lips quivering, at first unable to
make them say the words that lay stuck in his head. He saw out
of the corner of his eye Ferrapotti making his way to Der
Groot. "I'll have you know," he mumbled in a weak voice,
"that I am Australian, not American."

As if this were an excuse or even substantive reply to Der
Groot's powerful observation, indeed, accusation! Der Groot
waved Ferrapotti away, who adroitly changed course and made
his way to Dennis.

"Did you not receive your Doctorate at the University of
Pennsylvania?" asked Der Groot.

Dennis sat down in his seat, an act that helped calm him.
Ferrapotti was now approaching him from the aisle, still with
his grin, though obviously concerned.

In response to Der Groot's question Dennis rose again.
He looked at the Rapporteur who was flummoxed and did not
know how to intervene in a respectful way. The issue was too
controversial. He dare not get caught up in an argument about
race.

"You are right, professor doctor Der Groot," noted
Dennis sarcastically, "but may I point out that, if you do not
have valid data on the racial component of crime, and
especially of those who are in prison, how will you ever
determine whether the criminal justice system is racially biased?
Without such data, there is no empirical evidence on which to
develop policy that guarantees racial equality."

There, he had said it. True, what he had said was a paradox of sorts. In order to show racial prejudice, especially systemic bias, you must be able to show that in actual fact the bias exists, and for that you must collect data that profiles—dare one say the word—the race and other attributes of those who commit crimes, who are victims of crimes, who are processed through the criminal justice system.

Der Groot did not offer a retort. He assumed that all present would see that everything the young man had said revealed his racist view of the world, tat of he Americans, and the Australians, everyone knew that.

"Oh, er, oh," Dennis heard, in loud whispers in his ear, and smelled Ferrapotti's stale nicotine breath, "of course you're right. But you can't say it to these people."

Dennis turned to reply and thank his boss for the support, but Ferrapotti had already left and was on his way to whisper to Der Groot.

Buoyed by the support of his boss, Dennis stood again, and addressed the chair. He was learning how to make himself seem civilized.

"Monsieur Rapporteur," he said, "may I speak again? This is such an important issue in our times."

The Rapporteur, glad of a way to be included in this difficult exchange, replied, "the Chair recognizes Mr. Cotter."

"I have one small question to ask Professor Doctor Der Groot. Does he know how many ethnic Indonesians are in Dutch prisons, and are they over-represented according to their portion of the total population of the Netherlands?"

Der Groot stood stiffly. "As I have said, we do not collect such information. It is racist to do so."

"May I?" asked Dennis again respectfully addressing the chair."

"You may."

Ferrapotti was now hurrying back to Dennis with more

whispers, this time no doubt to tell him to shut up.

"Do you collect data on sex of the offenders or inmates of prisons?"

Der Groot pretended to busily write something down and did not respond.

"Does the delegate from The Netherlands wish to respond?" asked the Rapporteur.

"I do not," replied der Groot, clearly sulking.

"Of course you do," said Dennis, now feeling a rush of adrenalin that comes with winning. "According to your argument, collecting such data would be sexist."

Dennis smelled the nicotine breath. Ferrapotti was panting, no longer whispering. He squeezed Dennis's arm quite strongly. Dennis's cheeks were still flushed with the feeling of winning, though none present perceived the incident as such. But he then thought of the wonderful last lunch he had in Rome with his colleagues and new friends before departing for Strasbourg, and decided that such a life was much more important than winning a small argument.

He grabbed Ferrapotti's hand that gripped his arm and whispered, "O.K. I'll shut up."

2. KIDNAPPED

After the fall of Saigon in April of 1975, the cynics and critics of the United Nations, not to mention insiders who were well acquainted with the subterranean antics of Italian counter intelligence, so called, predicted that the United Nations Social Defense Research Institute in Rome, the baby nurtured by various politicians and top bureaucrats of the Italian government (such as it was, though any sensible person would also include the Mafia as part of the top governmental bureaucracy), would be short-lived, most likely a few years when what money it managed to raise from knowing or unknowing member states' donations, had been milked dry. Few could believe that the giant of the United States of America could have lost a war against a tiny, though as was now clear, dedicated band of communists.

Many blamed the US entrapment in Vietnam on the dalliances and incompetence of the CIA, given its pathetic history of failures, such as the Bay of Pigs disaster, and the near self-destruction of the CIA brought about by the incompetence of top spy Jesus Angleton who was convinced the Russians had totally infiltrated the CIA, yet was himself duped by his "best friend" Kim Philby who turned out to be a double agent. Fired by CIA director William Colby in December 1974, Angleton spent some of his early boyhood in Italy and was certainly closely linked to many influential people in the Italian counter intelligence elite (SID and its various ancillaries). Angleton was anti-communist to the core, and probably fascist as well, given his friendship with Ezra Pound. His role in Italian counter intelligence has never been seriously invest-igated. But there is little doubt that he laid the foundation for the CIA in America to establish important ties with the Italian Mafia, upon whose resources it would draw in the assassination attempt of Castro in Cuba, not to mention the assassination of JFK in 1963 by Lee Harvey Oswald, spied on when he was in Russia, cunningly manipulated and fingered by the CIA.

Necessarily, all of this is a long-winded prelude to the memorable day on which Ugo di Napolitano, Supreme Court Judge of Italy, and de-facto expert director of UNSDRI failed to show up at his office in Via Giulia, on Monday, May 11, 1975. He had not been in the office since Wednesday May 6. At first, no one thought much of it since the directors and experts who moonlighted from their other official positions in the Italian bureaucracy came and went as they wished. On Thursday May 6 the Director General of UNSDRI, who was not often in the office himself because of his "many diplomatic responsibilities" had received a call from the Carabiniere, asking to speak with Judge Di Napolitano.

"It seems that Judge Di Napolitano has disappeared," announced the Carabiniere. We just received a call from his wife who says he did not come home last night."

Director General Supreme, as he called himself when he answered the phone, smiled and said into the mouthpiece, "Oh, don't worry. I am sure he is on mission, often these are secret you know, as I'm sure you would, being of carabiniere."

The carabiniere said thank you and hung up. Director General Supreme placed the receiver on its base and reached for his car keys. No sooner had he done so than there was another call. He picked up the phone and said, impatiently, "I have important diplomatic business to attend to, do not allow calls to come to me unless they are urgent."

"Director General Supreme?" came a loud voice, the

sound of typewriters clanging in the background. "This is the *Corriere della Sera*. I understand that Judge Di Napolitano has disappeared?"

Supreme stood up and snapped his heels together as if saluting his troops. "I do not know who told you that, but it is definitely not true. I know where he is but I cannot reveal his location. He is on mission, as we say in the United Nations."

"His wife, we understand, called the Carabinieri. She's worried that he did not come home last night. Are you sure that this is a UN mission?"

"You are Italian, I presume?" asked Supreme, in an impudent manner.

"Well yes, of course I am, I am a top journalist for the *Corriere della Sera*."

"Then you would understand that men, especially those of highly respected status among Italians, have their, shall we say, dalliances?"

"You're sure of that?" replied the journalist, dumb-founded.

"Of course, but you should not print that. It is surely also a well-known fact that such relationships are well publicized Italian secrets, if you see what I mean?" Supreme joggled on his feet, itching to get out to his Mercedes, but proud of what he thought was his ability to frame in English, nuances and hints that hid the truth, as it were.

***

Next day, there was a small entry on the back of page 1 of the *Corriere della Sera*, mentioning that the Supreme Court Judge Ugo Di Napolitano was reported missing by his wife to the Carabiniere and that they were investigating. People close to the matter indicated that it was not unusual for Di Napolitano to be on mission for the United Nations for a day or two, probably staying at his holiday house in Fregenae, which was closer to the Rome Fiumicino airport. Of course, people close

to Di Napolitano knew that he was with his mistress, Sabrinetta, a buxom beauty from the Sardinian mountains, where,
it must be said, kidnapping was a routine affair.

However, over the weekend the *Corriere della Sera* received
a handwritten note that stated:

"Judge di Napolitano is our captive and will be tried in our
court charged with corruption and cruel detention of our
people, heroes and liberators of the nation. We demand the
immediate release of our three compatriots held in Viterbo
prison. If this is not done by Tuesday, May 10, if found guilty,
Di Napolitano will be executed according to our law."

The note was signed "NAP" (Nuclei Armati Proletari).
And over the next few days they released manifestos detailing
the "trial" of Judge Di Napolitano, this very much reflecting
the modus operandi of the *Brigate Rosse* (Red Brigade) that
reaped havoc throughout Italy in the 1970s. The details of the
manifestos were, however, made up. That is to say, they did
not accurately report what really happened. This not surprising
since the Red Brigade and its various factions had been, as was
later to be discovered, or maybe was already known by SID,
the brainchild of a well-known publisher and journalist.

***

Just across the river from UNSDRI lies the infamous
prison Regina Coeli. It is an unattractive stone building, as
older buildings in Rome go, dating back to the 17th century,
facing *Via Lungara* that runs from the busy *Lungo Tevere* and the
River Tiber. One can see it from the toilet next to Judge Di
Naplitano's office in UNSDRI. Known for its brazen acts of
terrorism, the NAP had taken over a small apartment just
down the street from the prison, reached from an alley that led
off the Piazza Trilussa. It was a one room basement apartment,
accessed via a winding stone staircase, recently renovated; that
is, everything was painted a bright white. Three scruffy,
unshaven, stocky men, obviously from the south, probably

Calabria or thereabouts, their demeanor sullen and sour sat at an oblong table, wooden and bare, scrubbed clean, its top soft and rough. Di Napolitano sat tied roughly to a chair, facing them, set back against the whitewashed wall.

"You are responsible for the condition of prisons in Italy, is that correct?" asked the slightly larger of the three, sitting at center.

Di Napolitano wriggled a little. Then spoke in his familiar, sonorous high pitched voice, loud and piercing. "You cannot get away with this. Give up now and I will ensure that you are looked after." He eyed each of his captors carefully, finding it difficult to hold back a grin. They reminded him of the Marx brothers, Harpo on his left, Groucho, the boss in the middle, and Chico on his right.

"Shut up and answer our questions," growled Groucho. "We demand that our three colleagues in Viterbo be released."

"Who are they?" asked Di Napolitano. Though he already guessed who they would be—the threesome whose escape from Viterbo prison had been foiled because of a tip-off from a Mafia confidant inside the prison.

Groucho responded. "Pietro Sofia, Giorgio Panizzari, and Martino Zichitella. If they are not released by the end of the week, you will be sliced up into many pieces and spread out over Rome's filthy streets."

One should add that there was a garbage collectors' strike, the direct result of the incompetent administration of the city by the current occupants of the city's administration, the Communist Party.

Unperturbed, Di Napolitano replied, "you may well kill me, but that will not get you what you want, will it? In fact, it will more than likely end up with you all going to jail forever. Or, if a fascist party wins the next election, you may even hang, if they bring back the death penalty."

"Are you in charge of the conditions and treatment of

prisoners in Italy's jails? Yes or no!" demanded Groucho.

"Let's kill him now to be done with it. He's not going to do us any good," muttered Chico.

"I am not in charge and have no authority over any prisons. I am simply an expert consultant. That is all," answered Di Napolitano.

Harpo stirred as if coming back from a deep sleep and said, leaning across the table, "if you are such an expert, why don't you recommend the abolition of all prisons? It's obvious to all of us that they are brutal, cruel places. Nobody, including terrorists or murderers deserves to be in such places."

Di Napolitano was taken aback by the intelligence displayed by this otherwise oaf, his very red face obviously the result of too much wine. "You have been drinking too much wine, my friend," he said haughtily, "you know that if you were in charge you would put your enemies in prison, that is if you did not kill them," answered Di Napolitano.

"I am not your friend. And you are right. It is better to kill your enemies than pretend to forgive them by putting them in jail," Harpo answered. And as if to drive home his point, he reached under the table and brought up a bottle of red wine and took a swig.

"I see," said Di Napolitano, "I see, indeed. I see that you lack courage, and find it in the wine. There are many terrorists like you." Had his arms been free, Di Napolitano would have waved them to drive home his point. As it was, his high pitched lilting voice, and sonorous Neapolitan accent, were enough to carry the weight of his intellect and, perhaps more important, his position in the Italian bureaucratic hierarchy. It angered all three of his kidnappers. They stood up as one, knocking their chairs backwards, and thumped the table.

And so it went on for three days of interrogation and presentation of "evidence" of the judge's guilt, the proclamations and reports of the proceedings conveyed to the press that hungrily consumed every word and printed them on their front pages.

The authorities, at first the director of Italian prisons, responded with the standard, "we do not negotiate with terrorists." But as the proclamations and threats became more and more violent, by the third day the person who ended up responding was the Prime Minister himself, Aldo Moro.

In the meantime, the apartment was beginning to smell of stale pizza and the toilet, a small closet with a rickety door that would not stay shut. All men were now unshaven and disheveled. The judge did his best to retain his composure as a Supreme Court Magistrate, but it was undeniable that his face was haggard from lack of sleep, which was difficult if not impossible to get, given the constant interruptions and questioning, and the severe discomfort of being tied to a hard wooden chair. So by the end of the third day, something or someone had to give.

Di Napolitano, his sharp intellect a little numbed, remained continuously alert for an opportunity or advantage to show itself. A sign of weakness was all he needed. Harpo now was frequently dropping off to sleep. Chico remained vigilant and kept muttering to himself to keep awake, stirred and stood from his chair and shouted at the judge, always with threats of violence, even getting so close with fists raised, but never actually attacking him. Groucho slumbered, occasionally grabbed Chico to restrain him from beating the judge, then snoozing, only to wake suddenly and pepper the judge with more questions, then sleep as he awaited an answer.

The resilient judge managed never to sleep, refused to look distressed. He stared at them individually to make strong eye contact. And just as Chico had made another death threat, Di Napolitano raised his head and spoke in his best magisterial voice. "Release me now and I will arrange for the release of your colleagues from Viterbo Prison," he said as if presenting the verdict of a trial.

Groucho blinked, Harpo awakened after a big snore, and Chico snarled in response. "Liar! Let's kill him now. I've had enough."

Groucho sat up. "You heard what that filthy piece of shit Moro said. He will never negotiate with a terrorist."

Di Napolitano replied with confidence. "That is right. He will not. But I will, and I am now. As my position as expert consultant to the Department of Prisons I can issue an edict for the release of any inmate if I can show cause."

"But what about Moro? Isn't he your boss?" responded Groucho, full of suspicion.

"Have you forgotten that this is Italy, and in politics no politician is anyone's boss. The politicians talk. We in the bureaucracies, the labyrinths of power, the complexities of which you could not even begin to imagine, anything can be done. And I mean anything," lectured Di Napolitano.

"I don't know. What you said, it sounds like bullshit to me," murmured Chico, clenching his fist and now standing threateningly right beside the judge.

Groucho blinked and fingered his heavy moustache. "You mean you can get them out?"

"Of course," replied Di Napolitano confidently. "I am very powerful in the corridors of prisons and courts. Is that not why you chose to kidnap me?"

Harpo snored again, then woke. He looked around with his heavy eyes, then stood and muttered more to himself than to anyone else. "Fuck this. I'm leaving." And when he opened the door to leave, the cool air of the night breeze and the sounds of people playing around the fountain in Piazza Trilussa wafted into their apartment that had become a smelly, disgusting cavern.

Chico stared at Groucho in disbelief. "You didn't stop him? What if he goes off and talks to everyone?" he cried.

"He won't talk," said Groucho belligerently, turning to Harpo, "would you?"

"You know the answer to that, asshole," growled Chico. "I tell you, if you let this piece of shit live, we're fucked. I'm leaving. Fuck you all."

"And we'd be properly fucked if we killed him. And to what end?" answered Groucho, now realizing himself, that their venture had been unrealistic and pointless right from the beginning. They had expected an Italian bureaucrat to plead for his life. Di Napolitano had outstayed them.

Di Napolitano saw his opportunity. "I state on my word as a Supreme Court Magistrate that I will order the release of your three colleagues once I am released from your captivity."

He was about to repeat his promise when Chico walked past him, pushing his chair backwards, though thankfully it did not tip up, and left the cavern. That left Groucho. He reached down to his leg and pulled out a knife that he kept strapped there, just in case he needed it. Di Napolitano stared at it, then at Groucho. "You wouldn't," he said, frowning, pursing his lips.

"I would, if I thought it worth it. But you're not worth it," snarled Groucho with disgust. He threw the knife at the judge and it landed softly in his lap. "You can take it from there," he said, "and see you keep your word, or someone will pay for it."

***

After an hour or so, Di Napolitano managed to grip the knife and cut his bonds. He staggered to the toilet, relieved himself, and splashed a little cold water on his face. It was drawn and haggard. He ran his hands through his copious hair and felt around for his comb, but it was gone. His captors had taken everything from him, including his wallet. With difficulty, he staggered up the steps to the door that led to the street. It was somewhere around late afternoon, he guessed. He went to look at his watch, but they had taken it. He sat down on the old stone step to gather his bearings. He could hear laughter and music coming from around the corner. The noise of traffic hummed loudly in the background. Perhaps there was the faint trickle of a fountain.

***

The famed criminologist Franco Ferrapotti, the co-director expert of UNSDRI along with his friend and compatriot Ugo Di Napolitano went, one hates to say it, haywire. He rushed into the Director Supreme's office without permission and ranted and raved, while the Supreme sat, cowed, fingering his car keys.

"Oh, ah, er… how could you do that?" Ferrapotti ranted. "Have you no sense? And all the time he's been kidnapped? And what did you tell the carabiniere? He was with his mistress? And you leaked it to the newspapers? His wife's in my office now, crying. *Dio! Dio!* What if they kill him?"

Supreme buried his head in his hands. "I was only doing my job," he cried lamely.

"Your job? Your job is to shut up! That's what your job is!" screamed Ferrapotti in harsh Roman Italian.

Ferrapotti ran back to his office. Phones were ringing all over. He picked up his own and immediately walked to the corner of his office and covered his mouth over the handpiece, looking sideways and beckoning to Andrea, everyone's secretary, who stood at the door of his office, to close the door, and to take Di Napolitano's distraught wife with her.

"Ferrapotti here. Yes. I know. Yes, I do know who it was, or at least I have a good idea. No. Don't know where he is being kept. But don't worry. I have my sources. Yes. I will find him. The carabiniere? No. They know nothing. Useless. Just remain calm. I will find him. I have my sources. I have my sources."

Ferrapotti banged down the phone, rushed out of his office, bounded down the steps, and out the door to *Via Giulia*, leaped into his Alpha Romeo, which was of course illegally parked right at the door. In challenging times, he always got in his Alpha and drove it round and round the block wherever he happened to be and sooner or later it would come to him what to do. It was as if his Alpha spoke to him. And many times, when he and his friend-come colleague-come nuisance, Di Napolitano had a serious disagreement, they rode round and round in the Alpha until it was resolved. This created quite a spectacle, since their voices carried far out of the car, though the words and secrets they held were not comprehensible. He drove down Via Giulia as far as *Via Dei Pettinari*, planning to drive left, past the *Casa Palotti*, then back on one of the many narrow medieval streets. Normally, he would not bother to look right or left, simply drive where his whim took him. Other cars, this being Rome after all, would have to swerve to get out of his way. It was the unwritten law of the road: first there first served. Every turn or stop or crossroad was a race. But he was so distracted with worry for his friend's safety, that he hesitated and looked right instead of left where he had planned to go. And then he saw a figure, stooped, but at the same time trying to hold his head up high, staggering over the *Ponte Sisto* (Sisto Bridge). He blinked, and stared. Someone behind him tooted an awful horn, others yelled at him to get a move on. He drove left, just enough to get a better look at the pathetic figure. Cars came from everywhere zooming down the *Lungotevere*, coming up behind him from *Via Giulia*, others trying to turn into *Via dei Pettinari*. He drove his Alpha, or maybe it drove him, whatever it was, straight across the *Lungotevere*, a suicidal act, especially as one could not drive over the bridge because of a chain stretched across the entrance. It was for pedestrians only. No matter! Ferrapotti stopped his car right in the middle of the road, facing the bridge and leaped out, waving his arms, screaming at the top of his voice, "*Consigliere!* Ugo! Here! Over here!" Yes, it was his friend and now what a big nuisance he was right this minute. The traffic on *Lungotevere* was choked to a standstill. Horns tooted loudly, people got out of their cars, shaking their fists, yelling obscenities.

At last, a carabiniere showed up, initially preparing to take Ferrapotti into custody and charge him with any number of crimes. But Ferrapotti ran, something he rarely did because of his rather corpulent condition, calling, "Ugo! It's you! How did you do it? Come! Let's get you home!"

Di Napolitano staggered some more, and with a great effort managed to reach Ferrapotti's extended arms, and he fell into them, sighing, "Ferrapotti, I never thought I'd get this close to you!" This was Di Napolitano! Even in exhaustion, he sees humor.

"*Come diavolo hai fatto?*" cried Ferrapotti, then lapsed into English for no apparent reason, "Oh…er…ah…How the hell did you do it?"

The astounded carabiniere recognized Di Napolitano. "Judge! I will call for an ambulance. Where are the kidnappers? Tell me which way they went and I will radio for a car. And an ambulance for you as well. You look like you need attention."

"Can't you see he's exhausted?" complained Ferrapotti. Here, help me put him into my Alpha, and I will take him to the hospital. And get all these the cars out of the way!"

Di Napolitano fell into the car, Ferrapotti beside him. He revved the engine, as if to say, "get out of the way or I'll run you down." The flustered Carabiniere tried to get the cars to back up so that Ferrapotti could turn his car around and move with the traffic. "I need to turn around. The nearest hospital is on *Isola Tiburtina*."

"Franco. I'm all right. Just need a good glass of wine and a small plate of pasta. Then some sleep. Let's go to the office. It's the closest, and we can send out for something."

Ferrapotti managed to turn the car around and drive back down *Via Dei Pettinari,* then into Via Giulia. He gunned the

Alpha, its front wheels screeching, and drove like a madman, his hand on the horn all the way, the tires skimming over the cobblestoned street. He pulled up in front of UNSDRI and was met by several of the *pezzi grossi,* as well as the security guard waving his pistol, and two young soldiers, probably no older than 18, their rifles at the ready.

Ferrapotti wound down the window. "Out of the way! Out of the way! I have the Judge! He escaped! Stand back!"

The security guard opened the passenger door and, annoyed that he had to put his gun in its holster, helped Di Napolitano out of the car. "Call an ambulance!" he yelled to the doorman.

Di Napolitano, with a superhuman effort, stood up straight, indicating that he was the boss. "No! No ambulance! I am good. Tell Eduardo at the Trattoria Giulia to send over pasta fagioli and a bottle of red wine. That's all I need to recover."

"And no one is to enter this building without my consent," added Ferrapotti.

Ferrapotti and one of the *pezzi grossi* helped Di Napolitano up the steps and down the corridor to his office. Andrea came running, tears in her eyes. "Oh! Consigliere, you're safe! I will ring your wife immediately!"

Thus ended this troublesome incident. The one who suffered most, probably, was Sabrinetta, who had remained in Fregenae, waiting for her lover who did not arrive, unable to receive any sympathy from anyone, friends or relatives, because her existence was a well-known secret, which in practice meant that she did not exist, except in the imagination of others.

3. A SPY IS BORN

The Englishman never did show up, so his wisdom and learning at the University of Cambridge criminology school never reached the United Nations. However, the project, as far as Ferrapotti was concerned was well under way, and had no need of the Englishman, given that he had hired a well-qualified Australian, who had taken his class at the University of Pennsylvania when he was a visiting professor there. In fact it was there that the idea, and subsequent Ford Foundation funding for the project on World Crime had first been explored. A bunch of very bright Ph.D. Students who came there from all over the world took his class.

For his part, Dennis, the scruffy Aussie, who ended up running the project, after what seemed a year or two, though time, he had learned did not seem to matter in this life, was still at a loss as to how to proceed. The Council of Europe meeting had provided little direction or ideas of substance to even begin to design the project. So he sat in his office, shared with a visiting expert from Iran, who did little but talk to him of how things in Iran were done, what a wonderful university he had attended in Iran before he went to Ohio State University, all of this as he laughed and smiled, such a happy person. His main concern was to find a good *trattoria* for lunch every day, which certainly made Dennis's life much richer. Lunch, at least for U.N. Experts was a three hour affair. Most often taken in one of the many *trattorias* or *hostarias* hidden away in the alleys around *Via Giulia*, *Campo dei Fiori* and the like. Iranians were just like Italians. They liked food, that was Dennis's incisive observation. And as each day went by, so did he.

Yet Rome in the days after Di Napolitano's kidnapping had taken on a somber outlook. People in the street seemed to be tense. They did not stop and talk to passersby as had been the practice, as far as Dennis had noticed from the first day he arrived. Perhaps this was aggravated, or even caused, by the garbage collectors' strike. There was trash lying everywhere, in the gutters, in any corner or crevice where the winds of Rome blew them, piles of trash in plastic bags making mounds in front of apartment buildings covered in graffiti, and especially in the front of restaurants that, naturally, produced large amounts of rubbish every day. As well, carabinieri appeared to be everywhere, on street corners, cruising in their Alphas or motorbikes.

While the kidnapping of his friend and colleague Judge Ugo Di Napolitano shook the entire staff of UNSDRI, Ferrapotti remained his hurried self, constantly stopping to talk with anyone who may pass him in the corridor, darting into offices, looking this way and that. His arguments with Di Napolitano were more frequent, and the Judge's voice reached crescendos like never before. His most common words that could be heard, maybe even out on the street were, "Franco! Do you know what you are doing? *Non fai niente!* Next time the kidnappers will kill me, and you too if you keep going on this way."

It was now almost three years since his kidnapping, and Di Napolitano's kidnappers had been caught, so to speak, their colleagues had been released, just as Di Napolitano had promised when he was in captivity. So it was a kind of twisted *quid pro quo*. Ferrapotti stood at the door of the judge's office.

"Si! Si! But don't worry! I know what is going on," Ferrapotti whispered so loudly that surely most of the experts in the UNSDRI building heard it. And as if to demonstrate his superior knowledge, he added, "something's coming down, and I can tell you it won't involve you or me."

"Franco! What are you saying?" cried Di Napolitano.

"Oh…ah…eh…Don't say anything to anyone else," responded Ferrapotti in English, looking over his shoulder, then all around.

Flabbergasted, Di Napolitano threw up his arms in alarm. "Ferrapotti! Franco! *Basta!* "

Ferrapotti grinned and nodded, as if to say, "I've got a secret and nobody knows it but me." He stepped back into the judge's office. And muttered, "don't worry. I know what I am doing. Anyway, I have to run. Have a special case in Milano."

Di Napolitano eyed him distrustfully. If they weren't such good friends, he would terminate him immediately, except that he wasn't his boss anyway. "Milano? What's there? I thought all your cases were in the Vatican?"

"That is true. Mostly, you know priests with, er..ah..oh.. Personal problems."

"Then Milan?"

"I have a special mission."

Di Napolitano eyed his friend with a mixture of amusement and concern. "Franco. I know you. You will get yourself into all sorts of trouble if you are not careful."

Ferrapotti inched forward a little into the office. "All I can tell you is that the Vatican has money problems, and for reasons I do not fully understand, the chief administrator of the Vatican has asked me to look into the dealings of one of their major bankers who is located in Milan. After all, it's Milan where all the money is, right?"

"But you're a psychiatrist. Not an investigator. And I am sure you know nothing about money!" said Di Napolitano trying to keep his voice down.

"True again. But psychiatrists are in a way investigators. We investigate the mind, do we not? And it so happens, I think that one of the Vatican bankers is having such trouble. Or should I say, has already suffered much angst. Then in English, "Or, ah... eh...oh... that his decision-making when it comes to finances is becoming impaired."

The perceptive Judge of the Supreme Court leaned forward at his desk. "I see. *Penso di averlo capito.* Say no more."

"*Ciao.* I will see you in a day or two." Ferrapotti turned to leave.

"Perhaps you are going to Sardinia?" called his friend with a grin.

"No time for that."

***

Ferrapotti stepped off the plane and at the bottom of the steps a young man, could have been his son, held up the palm of his hand on which was written UNSDRI. The man nodded towards the terminal and Ferrapotti followed. Once inside, the young man turned his head slightly towards him and said in a quiet voice, a slight northern accent, "I am Wolfgang," I will be your assistant for the day. The meeting, or should I say the announcement, will be made just before we break for lunch.

Ferrapotti grinned slightly and looked at his watch, and in English he asked, "oh.. Ah..you are German?"

"Not quite. Swiss, but my father was Italian, from Torino. But either way, we are of the same race, are we not?"

Ferrapotti was not quite sure what this meant, but he just nodded in assent. A deep blue Alpha pulled up at the curb. "*Dopo di te,*" said Wolfgang as he held open the door.

"Oh.. Ah...er... So you are a journalist for *Corriere Della Sera?*" asked Ferrapotti in English.

"I was, or actually I am, though for the past several months I have been the personal assistant to Dr. Gelli. He is an amazing person," answered Wolfgang in almost perfect Oxford English.

"Oh... er...ah..no doubt he is. And also very brave if I

understand correctly what he is up to," said Ferrapotti.

"I don't think bravery comes into it. He just knows what has to be done, and he does it, and we all agree with his goal."

"Of course. It is essential," said Ferrapotti with a frown. "But there are many road blocks, the Vatican being one. I take it that is why I was invited?"

"Well, probably, though I do not know. I try not to get too involved. I just carry out my boss's orders and I am so busy I have no time to think about what he is trying to do at any particular moment."

Wolfgang looked out the window, trying to avoid Ferrapotti's gaze. Ferrapotti responded:

"Oh.. Ah..You know, I think it is important that the United Nations understands the situation. But there are certain *colonne sotterranee* that would oppose and undermine all he is trying to do. And that includes the Vatican."

"Yes, we know about that. But the Vatican has very little power, and, well I probably should not say this, it is running out of money, and Dr. Gelli is the only person who can save it. The banks, you know."

"Oh… ah..si…I know all about that. One of my clients…."

"Shhh! Never know who is listening," warned Wolfgang.

The car turned into *Via Angela Rizzolli* and pulled up at the front of the *Corriere Della Sera* headquarters. Wolfgang leaned over, annoyed and tapped the driver's shoulder. "Not here! Go to the back entrance!"

Ferrapotti grinned. As the car pulled up, the door opened and a number of individuals, talking loudly and clearly angry, poured out, gesticulating wildly.

"It looks like we missed the opening," said Wolfgang. "Never mind. The important thing is that you are here and representing the United Nations." With that, Wolfgang leaned over and pinned a name tag on Ferrapotti's lapel, the tag simply saying UNSDRI.

They pushed their way into the building, against the crowd of people exiting.

"What's going on?" asked Ferrapotti, somewhat annoyed at being pushed and shoved aside.

"Oh, I thought you knew. Dr. Gelli has taken over the *Corriere della Sera,* and is bringing his own team to run the paper. Although I think that a good number of the lead journalists will remain."

Ferrapotti's eyes immediately darted this way and that. Who was who of those rushing out? And could those remaining behind be trusted? "Is he that much of a threat? That bad?" asked Ferrapotti.

"No of course not. You know as well as I do that he's not a fascist. He is simply a sensible businessman who understands money, who has it, who should have it, how to get it, and how to spend it," answered Wolfgang as he pushed through large double doors. "This way. Dr. Gelli is looking forward to meeting you."

They entered a big meeting room, a large oblong table in the middle, many chairs crammed in all around it, a terrible din of many Italians talking loudly and all at once, and of course, gesticulating wildly.

"Calma! Calma!" called Gelli who now stood at the head of the table, running his hand lightly over his plentiful greying hair. "Those of you who want to stay may do so, and in your current positions. I am simply replacing the top editorial staff. From now on, this great newspaper will report the news without communist bias. The communists must be kept out. You have seen what they have done to our cities, the violence of kidnapping and terrors they bring with them all in the name of equality."

Silence suddenly descended. Then it was replaced with murmurs and a buzz of excitement. Gelli continued:

"We have the Vatican and its bankers to thank for their

willingness to step up and save this paper, and quite frankly, save this country."

Quiet applause erupted followed by a light chant of, "P2! P2!" at which Gelli raised his hands and called "*Calma*! Hush! We in the P2 lodge do not look for loud accolades. We work quietly in the background. Now go back to your families and tell them that your job has been saved and that you will, beginning tomorrow, be reporting all the hews accurately and faithfully and without bias. Thank you! Thank you!"

Gelli left quickly by a side door. Wolfgang managed to pull Ferrapotti close enough to the door so that Gelli could see the UNSDRI name tag. Ferrapotti, thoroughly entranced, thought that Gelli looked at his tag and smiled, but could not be sure. In a flash, Wolfgang had left him and trailed behind his boss Gelli. Ferrapotti turned and pushed his way into the small throng of chattering journalists, showing his UNSDRI badge. Many were instantly interested in the United Nations and what it had to do with P2. Some disparagingly called the UN a great organization corrupted by communists, others that it was essentially a tool of imperialist countries that was built on the back of slaves, dedicated to maintaining white superiority.

The year was 1977, the year that the clandestine Masonic Lodge known as "Propaganda Due" or P2, infiltrated and took over the failing left wing daily newspaper, *Corriere della Sera*.

***

Ferrapotti stood in front of the *Corriere Della Sera* headquarters and hailed a cab.

"Take me to the Banco Ambrosiano and hurry!" shouted Ferrapotti.

"I hope you've got plenty of money," quipped the driver.

"How's that?"

"They're going broke, everyone knows that. But then you're from Rome, I can tell, so you wouldn't know," joked the driver again.

"Si, si. I mean I don't have money in that bank. You think I'm crazy?" grinned Ferrapotti.

The driver laughed into the rear vision mirror as he wove through the Milan traffic, beeping his horn continuously, waving and yelling epithets at motorists who were in his way.

Ferrapotti smiled and caught the driver's eye in the rear vision mirror. "Hah! I keep all mine in the Vatican bank, that's where all the money is," he joked.

"Si, si, I know. But I heard it's all going to the Banco Ambrosiano to bail it out."

Ferrapotti looked shocked. "How do you know that?"

"You'd be surprised what I hear in this taxi," he grinned.

"I would, you're right."

The taxi screeched to a halt, Ferrapotti paid the driver, gave a generous tip, thanked him for his information, and stepped out.

The bank was closed. He pressed and repressed the bell button at front, and after what seemed like an eternity, a small side door opened and an old man, looking well into his eighties, squinted at him through rimless glasses.

"We're closed. Can't you see the sign?"

"Take me to your boss, Roberto Calvi. He's expecting me," ordered Ferrapotti.

"And you are?"

"The man from UNSDRI." That's all you need to know. Go on! Tell him and let me in." Ferrapotti pushed past the old man and pulled the door closed behind him. The old man had no alternative but to lead the way through a maze of corridors until they came to a very large rosewood door, beautifully carved, and knocked feebly.

"Come!" came a gruff voice.

The old man opened the door and with what strength he had, pushed Ferrapotti through, and quickly pulled the door shut behind him.

"Doctor Ferrapotti of UNSDRI, at your service, Dr. Roberto Calvi, I presume?"

"Ah yes! How good of you to come all this way. I hope Wolfgang managed for you to stop by the *Corriere della Sera*. Very exciting news indeed!" smiled Calvi, "please take a seat over there and I will sit on the couch. That is what a patient is supposed to do, right?"

"Well, I don't think we will be doing any deep analysis today. And if we get to that, it would be best if you came down to my consulting rooms in the Vatican," said Ferrapotti in the best of bedside manners.

"You are the official Vatican psychiatrist?" asked Calvi as he tweaked his small mustache, pulled the knees of his pin stripe trousers up neatly between thumb and forefinger, and sat on the edge of the couch.

"Yes, they trust me. Many of the cases are, one might say, delicate. Privacy and secrecy in both of my professions are vital."

"Then let's get on with it."

"Tell me when you first had these thoughts," asked Ferrapotti, putting on his most serious expression, a deep frown.

"When I realized that the bank was *fottuto*."

"I see. So you have never had such thoughts before?"

"No, never! When you live your life making money, you have to be positive all the time. I always expect to make money, never to lose it, or if the latter, only temporarily, if you see what I mean."

"*Si, ho capito perfettamento*. Immediately, I would advise you not to stand by an open window that is more than two levels above the ground."

"Oh, no. I think you have misunderstood my problem. It is not the loss of money, although it will no doubt affect many people badly, unless the Vatican steps in and saves us, which I think they will."

"So this is not what is bothering you?"

"Well, not really. You have to take risks if you want to be successful in finance. And with banks, well, I'm just taking risks with other people's money, aren't I?" said Calvi, a faint smirk, the moustache rising a little as his upper lip curled.

Ferrapotti crossed his legs, his mahogany chair, though beautifully crafted, was a little high for him and made him uncomfortable. "Then why am I here?" he asked, his perpetual grin breaking out.

"I'm having…." Calvi looked down and wriggled on his seat even further forward to the edge of the embroidered couch.

Ferrapotti waited, raising his eyebrows, his tongue quickly wetting his lips in anticipation.

"… I can't, I mean, well, my friend…" stuttered Calvi.

"Friend? asked Ferrapotti, suddenly guessing what Calvi was trying to say.

"I can't…"

Ferrapotti leaned forward from his chair. He tried to look as kindly and understanding as he could. Empathy was what it was all about. "Oh, I get it. You have a male friend…" he said, deliberately not finishing the sentence.

"Yes, that's why Bishop Marcincus advised me to consult with you. But it's not exactly that. After all, my preferences in that direction are not at all new."

"Then…what?"

"I can't raise one. At first I thought it was boredom or that my partner was no longer of interest to me. But I tried others, and it was the same. A gorgeous young neophyte came on to me when I visited the Vatican last month, but it was no use. I wasn't up to it."

Ferrapotti worked hard to hold back a grin. Wasn't up to it! "Are you having dreams or fantasies of encounters?" asked the good doctor.

"Nothing. Can't sleep though. Try to think of past encounters, but nothing comes."

"Yes. Well. I can see what your problem is. It's depression, pure and simple, but exhibiting itself through sexual dysfunction, rather than in that other major symptom of depression, suicide," announced Ferrapotti with authority.

"Well, either way," said Calvi, looking down, "if I can't have sex, I might as well be dead."

"There is a new anti-depressant drug under trial that I could prescribe for you. It's popularly known as ketamine. They're using it in Vietnam. Very experimental though. It is essentially used as an anesthetic, but in very small doses, can stave off depression."

"If it's experimental, I'm not sure about that. Besides, I haven't had suicidal thoughts as yet."

"Perhaps it's not a good idea to wait for the inevitable. Depression is a very serious disease."

"That's why I've come to you, Doctor Ferrapotti."

"Then I suggest we meet weekly if possible in my Vatican clinic. It helps you know, simply to have someone to talk to about your problems. Unless you have someone else to talk to? Your priest perhaps?"

"*Penso di no*. I know these Vatican types too well. All they think of is money. And I do not have a local priest. I will try to see you once a week, but my schedule is so busy.

"Excellent! Here is my UNSDRI card. You can always get me there, even if an emergency," said Ferrapotti with a happy smile as he stood and reached out to shake hands.

But Calvi did not respond with a handshake. Instead, with tears in his eyes, he embraced his doctor in the Italian way, kissing each cheek. "*Grazie mille!* Can't thank you enough! This talk has helped me already. And if you need any financial advice, don't hesitate to come to me."

"Thank you. But I have most of my important finances and transactions done in Puerto Rico. That's just in case the Communists take over this country."

"Makes sense. Do you have American citizenship, then?"

"A green card. Just as good, maybe better."

Ferrapotti turned and departed, the old man was waiting outside the door to show him the way out.

4. THE SPY THAT WASN'T

Since Di Napolitano's kidnapping, the atmosphere at UNSDRI remained tense. Two uniformed militia men, young conscripts, stood at the entrance, their automatic weapons slung over their shoulders. This did not stop them though, from smoking and chatting with each other. The few cars that came by, usually dark colored government vehicles were made to slow to a snail pace and their drivers were questioned. Dennis found it very uncomfortable to come into the office, to be looked up and down by the several guards and various couriers, functionaries, and hangers on, as he bounded up the steps and into the great old building.

It was the morning of March 16 1978. It was a day that Dennis would remember for many years to come. As he entered the great hall, he heard the voices of his twin bosses echoing down the corridor. They were louder than usual, and he guessed that it would not be long before they went out to Ferrapotti's car to drive round and round the block arguing. Andrea emerged from her office looking distraught, yet dignified in her carabiniere colors. She turned towards Di Napolitano's office, but then looked away and came to Dennis.

"What's going on?" Dennis asked, "are you OK?"

"Haven't you heard?"

"What?" The fact was, Dennis never watched the news on TV because he didn't have one, and generally never even looked at the headlines of the newspapers. The whole world could be coming to an end and he would not know it. He was totally absorbed in the "*carpe diem*" of Italian life. Enjoy today, tomorrow may never come.

Andrea stepped aside as though to let Dennis pass. "Aldo Moro has been kidnapped!" she cried.

"Who's he?" asked Dennis, very much the Aussie.

"You don't know? He's the most famous politician, was the prime minister of Italy! They cornered him on Via Fani, shot all his guards and drivers and took him away."

Dennis stepped back into his office. "Oh! That's terrible. What is the world coming to?" was all he could think of to say.

Andrea hurried towards Di Napolitano's office. She met Ferrapotti half way.

"I knew this would happen," he said, "I told them so. They wouldn't listen to me."

Dennis came out of his office. "Is there anything I can do?" he asked.

Ferrapotti looked at him with his usual grin. "No...er...ah..." He fumbled in his pocket for a cigarette. "Got a light?" he asked.

"Sorry, don't smoke," answered Dennis.

"Oh.. Er... ah... He's had it. They'll kill him, you wait, I know those people. It's a Red Brigade faction. Di Napolitano was just a trial run. This time they'll kill their victim."

"You think so?" asked Dennis.

"Oh.. Er.. Of course, they will issue ridiculous demands. But you wait and see. They'll kill him. They can't risk keeping him alive. Besides he's an ardent anticommunist. Believe me, I know. I have very good contacts." Ferrapotti looked sideways and all around as if he were worried someone was eavesdropping.

Dennis looked around too, then realized how silly it was. "Will the carabiniere negotiate with them?" he asked trying to show concern and interest.

Andrea replied, "my father says that they will do their best but that there is a rule that they never negotiate with terrorists."

"Your father?" asked Dennis in disbelief.

Ferrapotti replied, with his biggest grin, "her father is Director General of the Carabiniere, and a very good friend of mine."

***

There followed 55 days of negotiations and debacles. As they did in the Di Napolitano kidnapping, the Red Brigade put Moro on "trial" the charge being, generally, that he headed an immoral, unjust and corrupt imperialist party (The Christian Democratic Party), and demanded that Moro be exchanged for a number of prisoners. Moro wrote a letter to the Pope asking him to negotiate on his behalf. In response the Pope gave a speech asking the Red Brigade to return Moro to his family without conditions. Moro took this to mean that the Pope had abandoned him because it meant that the Pope would not negotiate. Most journalists, especially the *Corriere della Sera* took a hard line.

Ferrapotti marched up and down the hall of UNSDRI talking to anyone who came by, informing them that the day chosen for the kidnapping was the day on which the PCI (Italian communist party) for the first time would gain an active part in the Italian government. Ferrapotti was so concerned that he had packed his bags and already sent his wife and children to Puerto Rico. He was sure that there would be a major insurrection any time now. As he said, over and over, he had his sources.

Di Napolitano, for his part, stayed away from the limelight, even though he was the most obvious one to consult, having had the personal experience of being kidnapped by the Red Brigade (though some argued that it wasn't really the Red Brigade but a different faction). He shrewdly refrained from giving any advice, saying that this situation was quite different from his own, since he was not directly involved in politics or

government, as was Moro. Ferrapotti agreed with him, for
once, though they differed on whether the government should
negotiate. In fact, unbeknownst to any of the UNSDRI staff,
including Di Napolitano, Ferrapotti, a psychiatrist after all, had
offered to negotiate with the terrorists, since he understood,
he claimed, their thinking. When this became public knowledge, Ferrapotti received a hurried phone call from his patient
Calvi warning him to stay out of it, that certain parties saw it
as a soft way to let the Red Brigade get away with murder, since
they had, after all, killed all five of Moro's guards and drivers.
Ferrapotti argued that he was not looking to go light on the
kidnappers, indeed, once he got them to give up Moro, the
government could do whatever it liked with them. He was only
interested in saving Moro's life. Moro did not deserve the death
penalty on any grounds.

In any event, no resolution could be found and the
kidnappers whether tired, confused or both, stopped communications. On May 8, 1978, Moro's body was discovered in the
trunk of a Renault 4, in Via Michelangelo Caetani, a tiny street
just around the corner from UNSDRI and not far from the
building that housed the growing Italian Communist Party.
Moro had been shot ten times.

"If only they had listened to me," complained Ferrapotti.

"There's nothing you could have done, Franco," cried Di
Napolitano. "Believe me!"

"I tell you, there's even worse to come. Mark my words!"
warned Ferrapotti.

"I know, I know, you have your sources," quipped Di
Napolitano.

"No, no. There is also a secret committee that I am
chairing, set up by Cossiga, Minister for Interior. We will get
to the bottom of this."

"What bottom could there be? What can you tell them
that they do not already know, which is next to nothing?" asked

the prosecutorial Di Napolitano.

"We can figure out what will be the next move of the Red Brigade," countered Ferrapotti.

Di Napolitano looked up from his desk, adopting his serious magistrate's expression as though delivering a judgement. "What is required is a tough, no nonsense prosecutor and then the courage to administer the required punishment."

Ferrapotti was about to respond when he suddenly thought that maybe it would be interesting to have a third or even fourth opinion, so he called out down the hallway for Dennis the Aussie and for Andrea to come.

Andrea came running of course, her notepad in hand. Dennis at first did not respond, as he had never before been called upon. So he waited a little until he heard his name called clearly, this time by Di Napolitano, whom he considered not actually to be his boss, but anyway knew that he had to respond.

The two appeared in Di Napolitano's office standing uncomfortably aside, while Di Napolitano sat back in his large office chair, and Ferrapotti walked up and down in front of the desk.

"Oh..er..ah..should there be a special committee of experts to assess the operations of the Red Brigade in the Moro case?" asked Ferrapotti.

Andrea did not hesitate. "They should all be tried and found guilty and then shot, just like they shot Moro!"

"You mean," said Di Napolitano looking a little superior, "that we don't want a committee, just a trial and its aftermath?"

"In my opinion a trial is not needed. Just take them out and shoot them," insisted Andrea. "The same way they shot the body guards, three of whom were carabiniere. That's what my father says anyway, and who could disagree?"

"Oh.. Ah..er.." Ferrapotti turned to Dennis, but just as he did so, a loud explosion, or crack of a gun, sounded throughout the corridor and office, and the noise of shouting followed. Di Napolitano jumped up from his chair, crying, "someone has a gun!" The noise of shouting continued, but there were no more gun shots. Di Napolitano led the way, taking big brisk steps. "The noise is coming from downstairs at the entrance. Someone must have tried to break into the building."

Downstairs at the entrance pandemonium reigned. The two armed military conscripts stood at the ready with their automatic weapons. They looked very young, blushing perhaps, and very frightened. Just inside the doorway on the cold stone steps lay the body of a well dressed young man, sprawled on his back, blood pouring from his chest, his eyes staring blankly, through his lowly flickering lids.

"What happened?" asked Di Napolitano, the judge, and proper person to take charge.

The official guard stepped forward, gun in hand. "I thought he was trying to sneak in. I told him to stop. He didn't seem to understand spoke some crazy language. He put his hand inside his jacket, I thought he was a terrorist pulling out a gun. So I shot him."

Ferrapotti called out "make way, move back! I'm a doctor. Get back I tell you!" He kneeled down to examine the body and felt its neck for a pulse. "He's alive, just! Call an ambulance!"

The body's eyes slowly opened, and mumbled, *"Ego te quidem Anglorum…"*

Ferrapotti stood back, aghast. He felt inside the body's jacket pocket and withdrew a letter typed on UNSDRI letterhead.

Di Napolitano took over crowd control. "Come on now, move along. There's nothing to see here. Give the poor fellow some air." He turned to the conscript soldiers, "come on now, get everyone moving away."

Dennis remained in the background, inclined to sneak back to his office where it was safer. But he had heard something of what the assailant had muttered. It was Latin, but he heard not enough of it to translate, though then again, had he heard it clearly there was a good chance that he would still not have been able to understand it.

Ferrapotti looked at the letter, then down to the assailant, whose eyes now remained open, dead.

"*Mio Dio* !" he muttered, "it's the Englishman!"

Dennis was aghast. He jumped down the few steps and pushed his way to the front of the onlookers. "Dr. Ferrapotti, did I hear you right?" he asked with timidity.

"Er.. Ah.. Oh.. That's what this letter says. It's the letter I wrote a long time ago."

"That makes sense," said Dennis. "Those Cambridge types all learn Latin, and that's what he was saying. He said, if I am not mistaken, 'I'm your Englishman.' He probably thought that his Latin was near enough to Italian."

Ferrapotti looked down at the lifeless body. "Oh.. Er..ah..Well, here is one more innocent victim of the murderous Red Brigade."

5. VATICAN THERAPY

In any mystery, scandal or crime, veteran investigators always say, "follow the money" and you will find the crime or culprit. Perhaps this is true, but in Roberto Calvi's case, it was not so simple. The fact is that he lived in money, it was his life. So when an investigation into the alleged illegal movement of some several billion lire from the Banco Ambrosiano, to an undisclosed recipient or recipients was commissioned by the Bank of Italy, Calvi was naturally targeted because he was President and Chairman of that bank. It is possible that the missing money might have been overlooked were it not for the fact that the bank was closely associated with the Holy See. And of course, the Vatican was a perennial target of far left politicians and various agents of the PCI (Italian Communist Party). In retrospect, after many commissions and inquiries, we now know that there were many other "parties of interest" involved in this alleged irregular movement of funds. Those parties included, but were not limited to, the CIA, MI6, the FBI, and Italy's various spy agencies: SIFAR, Armed Forces Information Service (Servizio Informazioni Forze Armate), SID, Defense Information Service; SISDE, Service for Intelligence and Democratic Security; SISMI, Service for Military Intelligence Security.

If there were any stalkers following Calvi therefore, he would have led them to the Vatican Library on a regular basis, once every week. That he would do this, a man so loaded with work and personal problems, find the time to come from Milan to Rome once a week and spend the afternoon in the Vatican was amazing; incredible that Calvi was physically and mentally able to find the time, incredible to his watchers who recorded his every move.

***

Dr. Ferrapotti's official consulting room was tucked away on the second floor of the Vatican library, between the Biblioteque Pontificale and Cortile S. Damaso. He was such a busy man, what with his students at the University of Rome and his research at UNSDRI, that he had no time for regular patients, so he confined his psychiatric practice to the referrals he received from the Vatican. He had developed a lucrative and very effective practice, essentially dealing with patients who were sent to him by the upper echelons of the Vatican, by far the majority of them involving problems of a sexual nature. At the time, homosexuality was a crime in Italy, punished by various amounts of prison time. Further, if prosecuted, the Vatican of course preferred to avoid the inevitable media sensations that would result. Dr. Ferrapotti therefore provided an essential service. He diagnosed such patients as mentally ill, unfit to stand trial, so the case would never reach the court, and his congenial relationship with the various prosecutors and judges he knew in the Vatican and even outside, assured that the case would be stamped "cleared." Thus the patient remained free, but usually required to meet with his psychiatrist on a regular basis, for a particular period of time.

One can see, then, that it was most unusual for Ferrapotti to have invited Roberto Calvi to come to him regularly for therapy (a vague word if ever there was one), not to mention that his office was inside the Vatican. The media and others, unspecified, would be watching Calvi like hawks, and undoubtedly report that Calvi had been seen entering the Vatican.

*

At the time, there were no privacy laws, so what went on between therapist and patient was not, technically, legally protected. This fact was actually irrelevant in Calvi's case, or any of Ferrapotti's cases for that matter. Ferrapotti was, as we have seen, a very talkative person, who loved passing on information, embellishing it, manipulating it, and exchanging it for other information he deemed necessary for his personal and professional life. Every sentence he uttered was laced with intrigue, and delivered in a loud whisper. Thus it was, when he responded to the light knock on the door to his clinic, he opened the door quickly, pulled Calvi inside, then poked his head out and looked up and down the corridor. He quickly retreated into his clinic and locked the door, turning a huge key in an ancient lock almost half the size of the door itself.

"Welcome to my humble clinic," smiled Ferrapotti in a whisper. "Make yourself comfortable on the couch."

Calvi, looking thin and a little haggard, smiled a little and sat on the couch. The decor of the clinic was hardly comforting. There was no window, only a faint incandescent light hanging from the ceiling,

"You can lie down if you want," said the good doctor.

"I don't know if I can keep this up every week. A lot of things are happening. I feel like I'm being hunted like a dog," complained Calvi.

Ferrapotti picked up the small wicker chair from beside his modest mahogany desk and placed it in front of Calvi. He sat down, his rotund weight causing the chair to creak. He then broke one of the first rules of psychotherapy. *Never physically touch the patient.* He took both Calvi's limp hands and squeezed them gently. "Roberto, I am your friend and counsellor. Tell me. Tell me anything you want. No matter. You will be better for it."

"Doctor, Franco, do you mind if I call you that?"

"*Si, senz' altro!*"

"You are a member of P2, right?" asked Calvi.

"*Si.* What of it? I only do it to keep up with what is going on. You know?" answered Ferrapotti.

"Yes. But I thought I was protected. But now I'm not so sure." Calvi looked away, as if searching for a window.

"What are you saying?"

"My bank. I think they're trying to destroy I," blurted Calvi on the verge of tears.

"My friend. Who? P2? They couldn't even if they wanted to! It's not really organized. Just a club, you might say,"

"Franco, I'm afraid you are very naive. It is now dangerous to be associated with P2," warned Calvi recovering his composure.

"What do you mean? Oh..ar..the communists?"

"Maybe. But there's a lot of others. They have infiltrated P2." Calvi looked away. Then back. "I tell you. I don't really know exactly. But I suspect either the CIA, MI6, SID or maybe all of them."

"But the Vatican. I thought you had a close relationship? They will protect you, no?" asked Ferrapotti as softly as he could.

"I can't count on it. I think they are after them as well."

"I don't understand. Why the Vatican?" asked Ferrapotti, probing.

"They are, have, you know how they helped before, saved the *Corriere Della Sera...*"

"But now P2 runs it, no? So you will be protected from the media, at least," said Ferrapotti leaning back, giving the impression of reassurance.

"Not here in Rome and everywhere else but Milan and even there I can no longer be sure. I may have to get away..." Calvi looked around the room as though looking for a way to escape.

Ferrapotti leaned back on his chair and it squeaked

appropriately. "Anyway," he said, "this is just a way of you avoiding what is really ailing you. Your, shall we say, trysts? Will you be calling upon anyone while you are here close to the seminary for young priests in training?"

"I think I had better be going," murmured Calvi, looking distractedly around, squirming a little on the couch, his face flushed.

"We have only just begun," said Ferrapotti, sitting further to the edge of the chair, once again reaching for Calvi's limp hands and squeezing them tightly.

"Let me go, Franco. I feel better already. It may have been brief, but it doesn't take long to lift the weight of deeds that have not yet happened." With difficulty, Calvi forced a smile.

"Guilt, you mean?" asked Ferrapotti with a frown, conveying his incredulity.

"Of course not. What's done is done. I'm sure you know that. But future acts, if you know of them. They can be pushed away and provide a narrow path to hope. The hope that they will not happen," mumbled Calvi looking down.

Clearly, Calvi was either confused or struggling to express himself in his depressed emotional state. Ferrapotti frowned some more. "Perhaps. But I do not agree entirely with your assumption that the past cannot be changed. There are many ways to cover up, falsify, construct counterfeit histories, perhaps you have indulged in those practices yourself? Some call it disinformation, at least that is what today's intelligence agencies call it."

"If you are talking about how my bank advertises itself, its public image. Yes, that is true. But when it is completely dam-aged, as is about to happen, the bank, even its false front, is beyond repair." Calvi his face the picture of calamity, struggled to look up, meet Ferrapotti's penetrating gaze.

"And you?" asked Ferrapotti.

Calvi, seaming startled, even angry, stared aggressively

into Ferrapotti's ever-blinking eyes.

"Ok. I completely understand," said Ferrapotti as he gave a deep sigh. "It's too bad these things are happening, because I was hoping to help you more with your personal problems of relationships, like we talked about before. My next patient who is due here any minute, was going to help us out."

As if on cue, there was a faint knock, and the door handle jiggled. Calvi looked anxiously at the door then to his doctor. He was about to get up and remonstrate, but Ferrapotti quickly rose from his wicker chair and opened the door.

Calvi couldn't help himself. The young priest was as beautiful as could be. He entered quickly and leaned forward, arms crossed as if to hold himself together.

"Michael. Meet Roberto. Roberto, meet Michael," purred Ferrapotti, in a soft whisper. He then quickly retreated behind his desk, leaving the two to stare at each other.

"I was just going," mumbled Calvi as he rose from the couch.

"Ok, my apologies. I am a bit early," answered Michael, a happy smile on his very white, Aryan face, his big crop of wavy blond hair dazzling Calvi as he stood rooted to the spot.

At that moment the phone rang and Ferrapotti picked it up immediately.

"Yes, OK. Definitely. Oh..ah..er. Good. Good. I will be right there." Ferrapotti looked around furtively. "I have been summoned," he said mysteriously. "One of my sources."

Calvi looked at him, and had Michael not been there he might have asked what sources. Instead he turned to Michael and said, "well I suppose I should be going too." He looked at his watch and said, "I need to get back to Milano."

Ferrapotti already had his briefcase packed and was on his way out. "Pull the door shut when you leave. It should lock automatically behind you, so make sure you don't leave anything behind."

A very excited Ferrapotti rushed out and away. He had been summoned to the Ministry of Defense to join a secret and select committee to review the causes and prevention of terrorism in Italy. As Italy's top criminologist, he would later tell everyone he met, he had been called to duty. However, an important factor that may have contributed to his selection was his membership in P2.

6. HANGING IN THE BALANCE

The select and secret committee on the prevention of terrorism met only twice over the coming year. One would have thought, though, that it was constantly in session, since the halls of UNSDRI were full of Ferrapotti's incessant talk, telling visitors and staff alike that he was off to his secret committee on terrorism. Not only that, he had a theory concerning the bombers. He was sure that one of the Red Brigade terrorists, possibly its main strategist, was a criminologist just like him.

Well, not ideologically, of course. He had formed this opinion after the bombing in 1972 of Giangiacomo Feltrinelli, famed publisher and activist, and claimed that it was his followers who assisted the kidnappers of his friend and colleague Di Napolitano in 1975. He insisted that the careful planning of the kidnapping, especially the communications with the Italian press, followed well known procedures of terrorist organizations, and that these could not be carried out successfully without contacts in the media. And Feltrinelli was an expert and owner of such media. Further, when Di Napolitano's kidnappers were interrogated, it was clear that they would not have been capable of carrying out the procedures by themselves. They had to have the help of someone who was much smarter and educated than they. One who understood the mind of the terrorist. He therefore suggested to the secret committee that it was most likely an academic, a criminologist in a university somewhere other than Rome. He was the top criminologist in the University of Rome and knew all others in the university very well, so it had to be a criminologist from somewhere else.

The secret committee listened most politely to his theories, but declined to act on them. One of the committee, whom Ferrapotti suspected was in bed with the CIA or some other intelligence organization, hinted that Feltrinelli's demise was not the accident of a clumsy attempt to set off a bomb, as was the popular theory, but that he was assassinated by some-one else. How could it be that Feltrinelli, a brilliant man, well versed in terrorist procedures, would blow himself up, when he had contacts who were bomb experts to do the bombing for him? And as well, why would he choose a power pylon that was on his own property as the target?

Ferrapotti did not listen to these criticisms. In fact, he never heard criticisms, because he was too caught up in his own theories, not actually theories, but simply talk. It was talking that Ferrapotti did all the time. Incessant talk. That was what drove his friends and colleagues everywhere a little crazy.

Yet, events that followed were to prove him right. Or seemingly so. His star patient, Roberto Calvi, while he did not manage to keep his appointments every week, did show up at least every few weeks for his therapy session. And on a hot and sultry day of July 1980, met Dr. Ferrapotti in his clinic at the Vatican. They sat as usual, Calvi on the couch, and Ferrapotti on the wicker chair.

"I'm afraid that this will be my last session for some time," announced Calvi, clearly in an agitated condition.

"You seem upset," said Ferrapotti, "what is the trouble? Michael has spurned you?"

"No, not at all, although I am upset that I must go away for a while, I'm not sure where it will be yet," said Calvi with an air of mystery, or perhaps resignation.

"Oh, I see. Something has happened?" asked Ferrapotti looking around the room as though he were concerned that someone was eavesdropping.

"Well, yes and no. They are after me, going to pin the blame for the collapse of the Banco Ambrosiano on me. There was money involved, lots of it. Some sent overseas, some coming in from unknown sources. I can show that I personally had nothing to do with it. But they will not believe me. I am sure of that. And you may have seen the leaks in the media."

"That you embezzled a huge amount? I read that and dismissed it as disinformation by someone," said Ferrapotti the therapist.

There was a light knock on the door. It would be Michael.

"Just one moment," called Ferrapotti.

"I just want to warn you. The CIA and MI6 are now involved. They have tremendous resources. I am sure they are targeting me, for some reason I cannot fathom," said Calvi.

"Now, Roberto, you're getting paranoid. Are you taking your medication?"

"No. I decided not to take it. Too risky. Besides it makes me drowsy and numbs my senses. And I need all my faculties as sharp as ever, otherwise I will slip up and the CIA or whoever will get me."

"I find this hard to believe. Are you sure of this?" Ferrapotti leaned forward from his chair.

"I am very sure. I must take my leave, you will not see me for some time. But don't worry, I will not succumb to depression. Strangely, now that I am being pursued, it keeps me positively active, no time for dark thoughts."

Calvi got up to leave. The faint knock at the door sounded once more.

"Coming," called Ferrapotti as he stood quickly and muttered, "please be careful. I am here to talk whenever you want." Then he added, unable to stop himself, "you know, I'm on the secret government committee on terrorism prevention. There's a CIA member on the committee, I suspect. I could talk to him."

"It's too late for that," Calvi replied. "Besides you may become a target yourself. But I leave you with these last words. Watch out for Bologna. There's something big coming down. It will convince you that I am not imagining all of this."

Ferrapotti opened the door to Michael who entered on tip-toe it seemed, dressed impeccably in a gray suit, carefully fitted shirt and tie. Calvi put out his hand and they shook. Then he turned quickly and left, putting his arm around Michael as they departed.

***

Ferrapotti, more agitated than usual, paced up and down the halls of UNSDRI, peering into Di Napolitano's office, going into every office, his voice streaming away. "I have to call a special meeting of the secret committee," he kept saying to whoever would stop and listen. "Something big is going to happen. I know. I have my sources." Finally, Di Napolitano came out of his office, put his arm around Ferrapotti and said, "Franco, you need some rest. Why not go home and have a good nap this afternoon?"

Ferrapotti stopped and pulled himself away from his dear friend. "It has to be a criminologist. There's just one. Of course, I know who it is!"

Dennis came out of his office, and Andrea too hurried up. The supreme Director had departed on mission, back to his homeland of the Congo. Ominously, he had sold his Mercedes just before he left.

"Ferrapotti!" cried Di Napolitano, "I have no idea how you have reached this conclusion. Be sensible. What evidence do you have?"

"I have my sources!" said Ferrapotti, defiant. "I must call

a meeting of the secret committee immediately. There's no time to waste."

He ran into his office and made several phone calls, none of them successful. The truth was that he did not know whom to call, as the secret committee always called him to notify him of the meeting. He tried calling the defense Minister Cossiga, but of course, could not get past his secretary. This, even when he shouted that there was going to be a terrorist attack in Bologna. He had also remembered the name of a criminologist in Bologna. It was Aldo Semerari.

***

At 10.25 CEST, August 2, 1980, a bomb exploded in the waiting room at the Bologna train station. 85 people were killed and some 200 injured. On August 26, Semerari and others were arrested and interrogated, but were released from prison in 1981. In 1987 many persons were charged and prosecuted in lengthy trials. There were convictions, followed by appeals. The trouble was that, as later became clear, the various Italian intelligence agencies (SID etc.), assisted by the CIA and MI6, conducted complex and successful disinformation campaigns, including counterfeit documentary evidence, resulting in arrests and prosecutions of right wing fascist operatives together with left wing Red Brigade operatives. Each, it seemed, impossibly masquerading as the other.

***

Ferrapotti enjoyed being right. He had partly predicted the bombing in Bologna. However, the secret committee never met again, so he was denied the satisfaction of being able to say, "told you so." He was, however, concerned about the whereabouts of his star patient, Roberto Calvi. He had received a note from Michael that Calvi was actually living in an apart-ment in Rome, but Calvi had not contacted him at all. Ferrapotti made inquiries of his sources (though the inform-ation was freely available in all the daily newspapers) and discovered that, in the heat of the various investigations and accusations made against Calvi in respect to his failed Banco Ambrosiano, and especially the apparent (though later "exonerated") involvement of the Vatican Bank, Calvi had disappeared. Investigators (we do not know whether one can call them "police") pursued him to Venice, thence to Zurich and finally London, where the trail ended.

Meanwhile, the "scandal" of P2 (*Propaganda Due*) erupted in Italy. Why right then, is a bit of a mystery since its existence was well known, though supposedly its members were not. However, in the course of collecting evidence concerning Calvi's involvement in the collapse of the Banco Ambrosiano, investigators once again visited Licio Gelli's house and found a list of members of the P2 secret organization. On the list were many top officials of public companies, not to mention key political posts in the government and out of it. One of the members listed was Franco Ferrapotti. Licio Gelli, the individual you may remember who briefly acknowledged Ferrapotti's UNSDRI name tag in Milano, was the purported head of the lodge. The members of this mysterious masonic lodge referred to each other as "*frati neri*" (black friars). It was Gelli, according to popular media, who was the real perpetrator of the collapse of the Banco Ambrosiano, and who had funneled the money into the Vatican coffers. Even today, in the 21st century, the list can be found easily on the Internet. Ferrapotti was then informed (actually it was Calvi's friend Michael) that Calvi had fled to London, where he stayed at a safe house that was provided him by Licio Gelli.

Then on Friday June 18, 1982, a person walking across Blackfriars Bridge in London noticed something hanging from the scaffolding beneath the bridge. The Police were called, and it turned out to be Calvi, hanging by the neck , his clothing and pockets filled with bricks and $15,000 dollars in various currencies. The death was ruled a suicide, according to

London's coroner.

When Ferrapotti read of the death of his patient, he immediately thought that it was consistent with Calvi's depressive state. However, the results of two separate investigations each 10 years apart was that the injuries to Calvi's neck were not consistent with hanging. Ferrapotti's sources informed him in latter days that it was of course, the work of all three intelligence agencies of the CIA, MI6 and SID and its variants. Why exactly they would collude to do this, and what if any Calvi's death had to do with the warring factions of terrorists from right and left did not appear to bother anyone. The media speculated that it and the major Bologna bombing were the result of the concerted efforts of all three intelligence agencies' disinformation campaign to undermine the authenticity of both right and left terrorists, especially left terrorists, and that the Bologna bombing especially, though actually probably, were carried out by right wing terrorists, but attributed to the Red Brigade and its ancillaries. Thus, by disinformation, the communists were defeated in Italy. It was not until 2020 that it seemed the actual person behind the Bologna bombings was none other Licio Gelli, according to the Italian weekly *L'Espresso*. But then, who could believe that?

7. WHO WANTS TO BE SECRETARY GENERAL?

Quite some time ago, Isaac Asimov proclaimed: "There are no nations!" Lauded as the greatest science fiction writer of all time, he was, and is, considered by many as a kind of fortune teller, that his novels often turned out to be predictions of the future of society and human kind. His claim that there are no nations was, of course, a statement of his own moral position that all peoples are equal, or at least ought to be equal. At the same time, though, he, and many who have followed in his footsteps (*Star Trek* and *Star Wars* for example) also heralded the idea of diversity, speculating on the enormous range of humans and humanoids and whatever living creatures that might exist throughout the universe, as yet unexplored. There appears to be no difficulty in adopting these two contrasting, actually, contradictory moralities of the future, often confused or blended into the present. If there is diversity—that is, each individual is different, unique—is not all such differentiation eradicated by the word equality? Ah, you say, I am playing with words. Indeed, I am, because I want to prepare you for the greatest quiz show on earth, maybe the universe, who knows?

The show is called, "Who Wants to be Secretary General?" and is aired every night at 6.00 pm and On Demand for people around the world on Australia's amazingly diverse TV channel SBS, that caters to viewers in all of one hundred and sixty-three languages. If you are a seasoned TV viewer of quiz shows, you will recognize that this show is a take-off from the blockbuster "Who wants to be a millionaire?" And in general, it does follow the format, offering contestants the chance to "call a friend" for help in answering a question, or to "ask the audience" for help. But the similarity ends there. For, as the promotional videos show, this is a real life quiz with real life outcomes. The final winner actually takes up the position of Secretary General of the United Nations. How, you may well ask, is this possible?

Until now, the position of Secretary General was selected by the U.N. General Assembly, subject to the approval of the Security Council. But over the years, after the appointment of nine Secretaries General, those countries not represented on the Security Council got together and complained that it was unfair that their choice of candidate was always rebuffed by the security council, dominated as it always has been, by the most powerful nations, generally those with an imperialist past, who have fought and won great wars both foreign and domestic. Why should such warmongers dominate the United Nations, an organization that is supposed to be the icon of peace and goodwill to all?

All past attempts to appoint a Secretary General who was brave enough to thumb his nose at the Security Council had been thwarted. It was time for a change, and this change was brought about by none other than Australia, a country not without its warlike blemishes (the destruction of its own indigenous peoples blamed on its imperialist mother England), having also dabbled in imperialism with its close neighbor Papua New Guinea, , but by and large had a tradition of towing the line with the big powers, especially its pacific neighbor, the United States.

It all came about in a raucous meeting of the Security

Council, Australia at the time occupying one of the rotating chairs. But the man behind the scenes was none other than Australia's gruff, ulcerous media mogul, the father of one-day cricket matches, Perry Smacker, and his U.N. Representative (well, Australia's U.N. Representative) Bevan Mudd, a former Prime Minister, much admired by the Chinese. In fact, Mudd spoke only Chinese in the meeting, refusing to speak one word of English. The very large Smacker sat immediately behind him, prodding him in the rear constantly, when he thought it necessary.

"Esteemed Members of the Security Council," began Mr. Smacker. "We are all well aware of the recent impossibilities of electing a new Secretary General. Some five nominees have been rejected, and the last meeting of the General Assembly was in an uproar, verging on bedlam. A number of members were carried off to hospital. Australia proposes an entirely new way of electing the Secretary General. We propose a contest, and the winner of the contest to be automatically appointed to the position, no vetoes allowed. We could argue about the merits of this solution, but we must face up to the fact that all regular methods of making the appointment have failed. We think that a contest, in the form of a quiz show be adopted. It would run for some six months or more, weeding out losers, and end up with a single winner who would be well qualified for the position. The questions would, of course, be asked specifically on the core attributes of the United Nations and its policies and practices. We have already begun to compile the lists of questions, and members of the Security Council as well as the General Assembly will be canvassed for questions. We will distribute the format for questions and answers at the end of this meeting. I thank you for your attention, and now declare this meeting closed."

Of course, the show was not open to just anyone. We could not have unsavory sorts participating. We must have individuals of high moral standing and who are comfortable working in a setting that is devoted to diversity in its extreme, which defines the United Nations, an amazing organization that seeks to understand, promote, and develop the ethnicities, cultures and economies of all nations, the ultimate aim being that all the nations of the world, all the ethnicities, come together as one. That one day there will be no super power or a few nations with huge economies. That all nations, ethnicities and cultures are unified into one nation, that no nation monopolizes military might, economy, or politic.

Finally, and perhaps the most pressing, is that no person who works or has worked in the employ of the United Nations is eligible for the position. This also includes the many consultants used by the United Nations. We are of the opinion that we need a fresh mind to steer the United Nations on a clear course, one that is not sullied by the deadening bureaucracy that the United Nations has become. We therefore have developed a check list of attributes that we seek from quiz contestants.

Of course, the obvious attribute that any candidate must have to be successful in our quiz show, is that they must be proven quiz show performers. Thus we have made a list of all those who became finalists in the world wide quiz show *Who wants to be a Millionaire?* and will use these obviously successful quiz contestants as the basic pool from which we will draw our candidates. That show is aired in over one hundred countries and many more languages. Indeed, the show is a wonderful example of bringing nations and languages together into one format, shared, and diverse. Every single version of that show features the now well-known final question, "Is this your final answer?" though, of course, each language has its own way of expressing this question. Each of these finalists was invited to try out for our quiz, the initial screening done by a check list of attributes, that the contestant had to answer, truthfully, of course. The check list is as follows:

1. Are you any of LGBTQA? Yes= 1 point
2. Are you white? No= 1 point
3. Are you fat? Yes= 1 point
4. Are you a gang member? Yes= 1 point
5. Are you or have you ever been a terrorist? Yes=1 point
6. Are you a rape victim? Yes= 1 point
7. Is your primary language English? No= 1 point
8. Is your primary language European? No=1 point
9. Is your primary language African ? No= 1 point
10. Are you or have you ever been an illegal immigrant or refugee? Yes=1 point
11. Are you married? No=1 point
12. Are you a university graduate? No=1 point

Candidates scoring above 8 are automatically accepted as quiz contestants.

The obvious choice for host of the first episode of *Who Wants To Be Secretary General?* was Eddie Squire, famed former president of the much loved and hated Collingwood Football Club, and perennial host of the Australian TV hit, *Who Wants To Be a Millionaire?*.

After many preliminary rounds conducted by hosts in the different countries in which qualifying candidates competed, the grand final was at last scheduled in Melbourne, Australia. The show opens with a door on which is inscribed a large old fashioned clock, the hands racing round and around to the dramatic sound of Beethoven's 5th, the ominous door knock. The door opens and out of the mist emerges Eddie Squire. He walks to the center of the stage and with his devilish smile in his most resonating voice says:

"We are excited to announce our grand finalist, multi-sexual, Francois Malkovsky II, from the Euronat permanent nudist community of France. If he answers the final question correctly, he will be appointed Secretary General of the United Nations, a position he will retain for the standard period of seven years, or less should he choose to retire, or be fired if he says or does anything that violates the equity and inclusiveness policies of the United Nations. We apologize in advance that Mr. Malkovsky is not black. He is, however, classifiable as "brown" all over, a result of his sun tanning regimen at the Eurostat resort. Also, I give those of you watching at home fair warning that because Mr. Malkovsky is from a famous and most respected nudist community, he will be appearing naked. Squire would have appeared naked himself out of respect for nudists everywhere, but our diversity and inclusion consultant advised us that it might be misinterpreted as his mocking nudists, cultural appropriation, as they say. After all, if Mr. Malkovsky were black, it would be shocking for him to color himself "black."

The music repeatedly blasts the first two measures of Beethoven, and Mr. Malkovsky steps through the door, all smiles. There are gasps from the studio audience as it gapes at the rather ugly naked overly tanned body of a middle aged man, somewhat over weight, his breasts somewhat enlarged, and his hips covered with a roll of fat.

"Welcome, Francois Malkovsky, may I call you Francois?" says Eddie as he offers his hand and Malkovsky shakes it.

"Thank you! I am very excited to be here."

"And Francois, I understand that you had a great deal of difficulty getting down here to Australia to participate in this first ever quiz grand final that furthers the spirit of One Nation World Government."

"Yes, it is difficult for we nudists to travel. We are forced to cover ourselves which is very intimidating. People gawk at us, you know, and some even make insulting remarks about our bodies."

"Well I'm sorry to hear that," says Eddie with his mischievous grin, "but let's look on the bright side. If you win and become Secretary General of the United Nations, you will be able to oversee world legislation that will allow nudists to go naked wherever they like."

"I look forward to that very much," says Malkovsky.

Eddie leads the way to the two seats suspended as though in midair. He ushers Malkovsky into his seat, then steps up to his own, suspended a little higher than Malkovsky's. "Are you ready to play, *Who Wants To Be Secretary General?*"

"I am."

"We have four questions. You will have thirty seconds to answer. You have two life lines in which you may ask for help either from a friend or from the audience. Is that clear?"

"Yes, perfectly clear."

"All right then. Here is the first question. U.N. General Assembly Resolution A/RES/217 A (III) Human rights addresses what issue:

A. Disabled people

B. Gender conversion

C. LGBTQA name tags

D. None of the above"

Malkovsky wriggles a little in his seat. For reasons of hygiene, the seat is hard and shiny. Certainly no cushion. "None of those," he answers.

"That was a quick response, Francois. Are you sure you want to go with that?"

"I am sure."

Eddie grins and frowns. "Is that your final answer?"

Malkovsky looks Squire in the eye. "It is my final answer."

Eddie leans back in his nicely cushioned seat. "Your are right! D, None of the above was the correct answer!"

The audience cheers and claps. Eddie continues. "You can stop now, if you want, and take up the lower position of deputy under-secretary general of the U.N. Food and Agricultural

Organization."

"No, thank you Mr. Squire. I want to be Secretary General."

"All right then. Let's go to the next question, this one for you to qualify as clerical assistant grade one, to the secretary of the current deputy under-secretary general of the International Court of Justice. Here is the question: The General Assembly Declaration of Imperialism Erasure is addressed in what document?

A. 1514 (XV) A/4494, Supplement No. 2.

B. A/RES/9 (1) of 9 Feb. 1946

C. A/RES/1514 (XV) of Dec. 1960.

D. All the above."

Malkovsky nervously crosses his legs and replies immediately, "all of the above."

"Now take your time, Francois, you have all of thirty seconds, you know."

"Thank you. But I spent a lot of time researching U.N. Documents. I know the answer is all of the above."

"You're quite sure about that?"

"Quite sure."

"Then it's your final answer?"

"It is."

Eddie looks around to the audience. He then looks back slowly to Malkovsky. "The answer is… D, all the above! You are right once again, Francois. You are on your way to Secretary General."

Malkovsky uncrosses his legs. "Let's get on with it," he grins.

"You can stop now, if you want," says Eddie, looking serious. "A position at the U.N. F.A.O. Is quite a good appointment. And it would be for life, so I am told."

"No, Mr. Squire. I want to be Secretary General. No good settling for less."

"All right. Then let's proceed. You are now two questions away from becoming U.N. Secretary General. Are you ready, Mr. Malkovsky?"

"I am ready."

"One Nation World Government is addressed in which of the following documents:

A. Secretary-General's remarks at the World Government Summit with Q&A.2017.

B. Eichelberger: World government via the United Nations. 1948.

C. World Government Summit hosted by Sheikh Mohammed bin Rashid Al Maktoum. 2017.

D. All of the above.

Malkovsky takes his hands from his lap, where they had been most of the time, and runs them through his greying hair.

"Thirty seconds starts now!" says Squire.

"I think I would like to ask my partner," says Malkovsky.

"Are they in the audience or do you want to phone?" asks Squire.

"My partner could not join the audience because they would not let them sit in the audience naked. I would like to phone The U.N. Vienna, where Sheehee is sitting hidden in the U.N. Archives kept there."

"As you wish!" says Eddie. He presses a button, an image of a phone is projected on a screen behind them, then someone answers. We do not see an image of the recipient of the call. Just a shadow.

"Oui allo ?"

"Is this SheeHee?" asks Squire.

"Qui appelle s'il vous plait, Yes, it is. Who is this, please?"

"This is Eddie Squire from *Who Wants to be Secretary General.* Your partner would like your help."

"Allo? Sheehee?" asks Malkovsky. "Are you watching?"

"Oui. sur mon téléphone."

"I think the answer is D All the above," says Malkovsky. "The trouble is I can remember no official U.N. Documents that refer to these topics. They must be speeches or other unofficial documents," says Malkovsky with a frown, clearly worried.

"Mr. Squire. Must the answers be in official UN documents?" asks Shehee.

"I am sorry, but I am not allowed to add or answer any questions directly bearing on the various answers," says Squire in a most formal manner.

"I am inclined to D," says Malkovsky, "because ABC are all similar."

"But it might be none of them," says Sheehee, in highly accented English.

"If it were, then that would be an option, wouldn't it?" muses Malkovsky.

"Je m'excuse. Je ne sais tout simplement pas quelle est la meilleure réponse," says Sheehee.

"Five seconds to go!" interjects Squire.

"Then D, all the above," says Malkovsky, head in hands.

"That's your final answer?" asks Squire, grinning and frowning.

"Yes. That's my final answer."

Squire looks down, the smile on his face gone. Silence intensifies. The audience shuffles. He looks up, then announces:

"The answer is D. You are right, and you are now qualified to be appointed personal secretary to the undersecretary's deputy assistant of the UN representative to the World Trade Organization."

Relieved, Malkovsky leans back in his hard seat, the surface sticking uncomfortably on to his naked bottom. Eddie Squire continues.

"You may stop now and enjoy a wonderful career as the United Nations representative dealing with the World Trade

Organization, or you may go on to the final question."

"Let's go for it!" says Malkovsky, shaking his fist, and jumping up and down on his seat.

Squire turns to the audience. "Audience, are you ready?"

The audience cheers and claps in response.

"All right, then. Here we go. Are you ready, Mr. Malkovsky?"

"I am ready!"

"Which of the following policy topics is NOT essential to world governance by One Nation?"

A. Inclusion

B. Diversity

C. Happiness

D. Inequality

"Mon Dieu! What is this One Nation? Did you not mean United Nations?" cried Malkovsky.

Eddie Squire remains silent. He looks down, then out to the audience. Then he says, "You have one help left. You could ask the audience. You have thirty seconds, starting...."

"OK. Ok. I will ask the audience, please," says Malkovsky running his hands through his hair, and crossing his legs.

Squire looks out to the audience. "Mr. Malkovsky, the next secretary general of the United Nations needs your help. Audience, your remote answer box is activated. When I say 'Answer" press A, B, C, or D button to send your answer to Mr. Malkovsky."

The audience stirs excitedly, and loud thumping music plays as the lights flash on the big board hanging above the heads of Malkovsky and Squire. The results were not helpful. Twenty five percent for A, same for B, Twenty eight percent for C, and twenty two percent for D.

Eddie Squire looks at the audience and then to Malkovsky. "You have thirty seconds starting now!"

Malkovsky uncrosses and crosses his legs nervously, "I

don't know, it could be D inequality, but I'm sure that the U.N. favors equality. I'm going to have to guess. Happiness. What is that? Maybe the audience knows better than do I. OK. Happiness it is."

"Is that your final answer, Mr. Malkovsky?" asks Squire, a serious frown, and still that small grin.

"Yes, C, happiness. My final answer!" Malkovsky pushes back on his chair and uncrosses his legs. The audience titters as it gawks at the contestant's nudity. He appeared at that moment, incredibly vulnerable.

Eddie Squire, enjoying the suspense, surveys the audience and tries not to look at Malkovsky's male body. "Would you like to change your mind?" He asks with his devilish grin.

"No! No! I have made my decision!" cries Malkovsky. The audience titters once more.

"The answer is…" Squire hesitates for effect, "…C, Happiness! You have won the grand prize and will become immediately we close this session tonight, the tenth Secretary General of the United Nations!"

The audience erupts into cheers and applause, Malkovsky jumps up and raises both fists, and dances around the stage, prancing full on to the audience. Fortunately, the show was not aired live, so there would be time to insert a warning to the viewing audience that the show included partial and complete nudity.

France hailed Francois Malkovsky as their greatest international achievement ever. Statues were erected in many towns, and an outsized one in Paris right next to the grand Egyptian Obelisk on the Place de la Concorde. This turned out to be a mistake, and probably marked the beginning of an underground movement to remove Malkovsky from office. The huge nude statue of Malkovsky was placed in such a way that, viewing it from the East the obelisk appeared as Malkovsky's giant erection. This was, of course, not by design, but either way, came to represent all that Malkovsky's administration stood for. Besides, the U.K., still bruised from its crazy Brexit, blaming especially France for making it so difficult, began a not so secret campaign to replace Malkovsky with Boris Johnson, as soon as he stepped down as Prime Minister.

Nor was the third world happy with yet another imperialist in the top U.N. job. However, those rising and emerging nations continued to squabble among themselves, so were unable to mount a successful campaign to unseat Malkovsky. Besides, they had never had a Secretary general who was stark naked, just like many of the third world's ordinary, oppressed citizens. The Russians and the Chinese also made feeble attempts to make Malkovsky's life difficult, beginning a campaign to move the United Nations Head-quarters to a much colder climate in Mongolia. As it was, people everywhere marveled at how this new Secretary General tolerated the cold winters of New York. It was rumored that he in fact, during the entire winter in New York, never stepped out of his office. This was not true, of course. But what was true, and struck a chord with the many developing nations that happened to inhabit areas of the world that were temperate and hot, was that Malkovsky had begun an immediate effort to move the U.N. H.Q. to Fiji somewhere in the Pacific. Besides, Malkovsky argued, he wanted the United Nations to reside in peace, thus his choice of the Pacific Ocean.

But what Malkovsky failed to sense was that, even though he had made great efforts to promote inclusiveness and diversity in the United Nations, it was not enough. On his first day in office he proudly announced that his administration would be completely open and transparent, and ruled that from that day on, all workers and consultants to the United Nations (which meant just about everyone, since it was by consultants that the U.N. conducted most of its everyday activities), would be naked, the only dress allowed was tattoos and painted nails. Many hailed this as a brave and exciting edict. But it soon became apparent that those who embraced this policy were those with beautiful bodies, or so they thought. When this awkward fact was brought to Secretary General's attention, he quickly announced that the words "fat" and "ugly" were never to be used and must be replaced with "shapely" and "gorgeous." Many other difficult, really just small details, but for some reason seemed overwhelming, bothered and annoyed his administration. All the seats in the meeting rooms and the general assembly had to be redone, so that people's bottoms did not stick to the shiny surfaces. They also had to be heated, because many complained that the hard shiny seats were cold. But by far the most difficult problem for Malkovsky's administration lay more deeply in the subconscious of his staff and consultants.

Meetings mark the manner in which the life of the United Nations had always gone forward. Meetings, large and small, assemblies, all of these require lots of people in one place, all drafting policies and statements, all arranging further meetings to consider the accomplishments of previous meetings. It was the small meetings, however, that marked the eventual downfall of the 10th Secretary General. These meetings occurred in small rooms, all seated around tables arranged usually in a rectangle, sometimes in a circle.

The U.N. Security Council had been quietly taken over by the gender dis-advocates, as they called themselves. And while the Security Council still held a veto power over the General Assembly, it was in fact through that council's manipulations and sheer brutality of language, that the important decisions of the United Nations were made. The important fact was—and this is an amazing eventuality that is completely in line with the grand ideals of the United Nations, all nations to put aside their differences and be united into One Nation—that gender differences be eradicated, or if not possible, be treated as small and inconsequential matters. People in the U.N. therefore were no longer to refer to each other by gender. Because English was the only language that had the flexibility of using pronouns in reference to people of gender—yet did not imply their gender—it was ordained by the Secretary General, that English was the only official language of the United Nations, and the languages of all other nations unacceptable until they had erased all gendered pronouns, nouns and matching adjectives, from their languages. A new United Nations Language Board of Control was set up to receive applications of languages that had been revised according to the U.N. Guidelines. In most cases, however, the Language Board strongly recommended that the easiest and simplest way to solve the gendered language problems was to simply adopt English as the national language.

You can imagine how outraged the French were when they heard of this new edict, coming from one of their own, no less! He had to be dealt with, and severely. They may not be able to cut off his head according to tradition, but maybe there was another way, given the modern techniques of personal destruction now available to all.

As is usual in clandestine operations, various competing, indeed, infighting factions arose among the gender dis-advocates. In the name of transparency, many meetings passed motions of diversity and inclusiveness that required surv-eillance cameras to be installed in every nook and cranny, wherever there were meetings, formal and informal. The French undercover agents saw this as a perfect opportunity to take down yet another corrupt French sovereign, to whom they referred as King (yes, the strongest gendered term in the English language) Malkovsky II. To think that one of their own would destroy their country by blithely abolishing its language!

The opportunity inevitably arose in a small meeting

chaired by Malkovsky, in the anteroom next to his office on the 38th floor of the United Nations building that offered a stunning view of the East river. He had called the meeting of his immediate staff, planning to inform them that he was so pleased by their performance that they would be receiving a ten percent increase in their salaries. There were twelve staff, including his personal driver, the only one who had complained directly to him, that he caught a very bad cold having to get out of the warm limousine to open the door for him when there was a blizzard. Malkovsky had ignored him.

Yet the first move was not made by the driver. Instead it came from one of his secretaries, Philomena, a sweet little thing, by Malkovsky's standard—a thing she was-- with a most inviting body, and a wonderfully inviting smile. He liked it especially when she spoke, which was constant, she was a real talker, from Rome after all, wagging her head from side to side, a bright blue eyes lighting up her face. Always happy. Or so it seemed. He should have known, however. She was Italian, that much he knew. And the Italians were incensed at him also, because their language was thoroughly debased by his edict that there were to be no gender pronouns or nouns. All were to be abolished. It left the Italians without any names or basically any nouns, unless all agreed on a word ending that was neuter. Already several governments had fallen in Italy because no agreement could be found as to the neuter endings of nouns.

Malkovsky sat at his seat at the middle of the oblong table. He surveyed his staff, all of them of course naked as was his edict. And on this day, his eyes briefly settled on Philomena as she lowered herself, chatting away to her friend next to her, smiling and happy. As she sat, she leaned forward a little and her smoothly shaven breasts seemed to stand out, the nipples he was sure were calling to him. He quickly sat down and tried to focus on the bodies of others around the table. But it did not help. His eyes came to rest on Philomena. He looked down at his notes, hoping that it would go away. His driver coughed a throaty cough, he was still getting over his cold. And he shivered from the cold air conditioning, or a fever. All stared at him. The pandemic was not quite over. Malkovsky gave him a disapproving look, and the miserable driver departed, hugging himself, trying to keep warm.

The meeting proceeded as planned, the gorgeous Philomena more or less taking over the agenda, making eyes at her boss, who sat enthralled, unable to do anything but grin a most salacious grin. The staff were most pleased at the promise of an increase in their salaries.

***

The brief meeting concluded after two hours, a short meeting by U.N. standards. And no sooner had Malkovsky returned to his office, when the computer screens of all those whose position in the U.N. qualified them to have their own computer in their office, were lit up by a surveillance video. Immediately he saw it, he knew he was done for. Right there, on the screen was the image of his very own penis, gradually raising its beautiful head. The surveillance cameras installed under the table had caught him in his moment of weakness, or was it uncontrolled strength?. And immediately his very own de-gendered undercover agents entered his office, unannounced, followed by his favorite little secretary Philomena. And then again, he felt a little twinge between his legs.

Philomena stood just inside the door. "That's him! She shouted! He raped me! It happened in our meeting just minutes ago! You can see the evidence for yourselves. Look at his disgusting erection! I saw him looking at me. It was awful! I felt like a piece a meat! And I just had to sit there while he looked at me and raped me!"

Malkovsky was read his rights of which there were none, as the U.N. had legislated that there was no defense against an accusation of rape. Besides the evidence was all there on the video.

However, the story does have a happy ending, of sorts. Malkovsky was not tried in a criminal court. He had insisted that all infractions were to be dealt with as mundane administrative infractions, the punishments to be appropriate to the "crime." In his case, once the U.N. had settled down into its old routine, his "punishment" was that he was never again to appear in public (defined broadly) naked. He must be fully clothed for the rest of his life. And as a side-effect of this scandalous behavior, all surveillance cameras were removed throughout the United Nations offices. The arguments about official languages and the degenderization of languages did not go away, however. All U.N. meetings everywhere and every minute of the day were taken up with this vexing and most complicated problem.

The hit quiz show *Who Wants to be Secretary General?* Continued, and became an annual hit. However the guidelines for its format were rewritten forbidding nudity of the slightest amount of any contestants and show host, though the studio audience and those viewing at home were excepted from this regulation.

8. COUPLES

To be honest, the true story of Noah's Ark has never been told. At least, that is what we now know after the finding of more fragments of the Dead Sea scrolls announced in March of 2021. After many hours of deciphering and putting together the jig-saw puzzle of the fragments, we slowly began to realize that the fragments we found were in fact a retelling of the story of Noah's Ark. In a retelling, we admit, there may be some embellishment. But we ask you to bear with us while we recon-struct the story to the extent that the fragments allow. Carbon dating, by the way, suggests that these fragments date well before the bible, old testament that is, as we know it. This story predates the bible, probably by several thousand years. But the measurement of time so distant remains malleable, something like a time fog. We walk into it at our own risk, arms extended, eyes lost in time, feeling our way with each uncertain step.

A further—embarrassing to some —difficulty is that there is much argument over what the ark looked like, how big it was, and, horror of horrors, there is no way such a boat could fit all God's species. Not to mention that the pundits of history insist that the number that got off the boat after the terrible flood subsided, was the same number as got on. Are you kidding me? Especially as they were on the ark for whatever number of years, how is this humanly or earthly possible?

The preoccupation of experts with the size, structure and building of the ark blinded them to what is by far the most impossible, certainly hugely challenging problem, of how to actually select and process the candidates for entry into the boat. Here are just a few small details. We know that there are countless species of life in our world, from plants and insects, to birds, animals and humans, not to mention microbes. Indeed, we can assume that in biblical times they had not yet discovered microbes as individuals, but rather only knew them as plagues sent by Gods of one kind or another, to punish humans for their existence. Just imagine the chaos. Every living thing learns of the impending disaster of the biggest flood ever to occur (in the past or future what's more), so wouldn't they all be clamoring to get on the boat?

Indeed, they were. And that is why Noah in his wisdom (obviously guided by God) immediately hired the best bureaucrat he could find, whose name was Damascus, who founded the city of that name. That's right, who begat, and begat, and begat after many thousands of years, the eventual progeny John Damascene, who became the Chief financial officer to the Caliph of Damascus.

And Noah said to Damascus: "I need you to select as many couples up to about three hundred, as I will be able to fit on my boat."

"How big is the boat?" asked Damascus.

"I won't know until I've built it," said Noah, impatiently.

"You must have some idea," complained Damascus, looking at Noah, trying to discern what was going on in that head, ninety percent of which was covered by hair, whiskers and a beard growing in all directions.

"Honestly, I don't know yet. I'm waiting on instructions," said Noah impatiently.

"From whom, may I ask?"

"You may not," snapped Noah. "I prayed last night, and

I usually get an answer after a few years."

Damascus rubbed his closely shaven chin. "You must have some idea, even a rough ballpark figure would help."

Damascus wanted to tell his boss to get his hair done and have a shave. But he resisted. He was beginning to regret having taken on this impossible task.

"All I can say is that there have to be couples, male and female couples, all from different kinds," muttered Noah, annoyed by this fastidious bureaucrat.

Damascus turned away, grumbling, "All right, I'll see what I can do. But you better hurry up with more information, or I'll…"

"You'll what?" asked Noah, shaking his hammer, clearly a threat.

"Never mind," called Damascus as he hurried away into the small town, if that is what it was, more like a honeycomb of caves.

Noah dropped his hammer and fell down onto his rough, leather-like knees, to pray yet again, though it was probably only five minutes since his last effort.. Surely he must get an answer soon.

In fact, no sooner had he dropped on his knees than a huge flash of lightning struck the rock beside him, accompanied by a few drops of rain.

"Count the drops and you will have your answer!" came a voice from somewhere inside his head.

And so Noah counted. And counted. And counted. He made it up to one thousand and sixty nine, but then had to stand up because his knees were hurting, then lost count and had to guess what number he was up to.

***

Damascus hurried to the caves, looking inside, trying to see how many beings were in there, asking any couples who were there to come forward. All he found were scruffy humans, a snake or two, though no snake couples. This was going to be a challenge, he could see. It would require expert organization and most of all, an effective way to communicate the availability of a free ride on the only boat that will be afloat when the great flood arrives. And who would believe that the flood will be so big that it will drown everyone and everything? Was that really going to happen? Damascus decided that he needed another information gathering interview with Noah, whose communication skills seemed wanting.

After doing the rounds of the caves, followed by a scribe he had hired on the promise that he would be allowed on the boat when the flood came, so long as he was accompanied by a partner making an acceptable couple. He described the couples to the scribe and their general location identified by an X he had made on a rough sketch of the cave locations. He could see that this was not a sensible way to record this information, so he immediately set about numbering all the caves and giving names to the inhabitants. Many did not have names, they just referred to each other as "this," or "that" and pointed. The snakes kept biting at his heels until he stamped on one and warned that if they did not behave he would not select any couples from snakedom. That had an immediate effect, and to his amazement, the snakes quickly proffered up a few couples of different looking snakes, pythons, tigers, adders etc. Those are the names Damascus gave them. But he had heard that there were many more strange animals, big ones with four legs, some with long noses, or long necks, striped, and of course there were birds, some of them he had seen roosting way up the top of the cliff, eagles or something like that he called them, huge things that swooped down on the snakes and gave them a terrible life in constant danger of being grabbed up and eaten.

Damascus turned to his scribe. "You need to go off to the jungle and see what else you can find. Spread the word that

Noah is prepared to take legitimate couples only — that is, male and female couples—no hermaphrodites or whatever. Just keep it plain and simple. And if anyone argues, strike them off the list."

"What if they don't want to come? I mean, who would want to get on a boat for who knows how long, maybe several lifetimes if what you say Noah said is true?" asked the scribe.

Damascus looked at his scribe, now well washed and shaven, according to his orders. "You have to tell them all that a huge flood is coming, so big, according to Noah, that it will drown everyone and everything in its path. That should scare them."

"But if what you said Noah said that he hasn't got room for everyone, only one couple of a kind, we'll have a riot on our hands with everyone wanting to get on the boat," complained the scribe.

"Scribe," sighed Damascus, "please do as you are told, and let me worry about the rest."

The scribe, hunched over and frightened of his boss, trotted away mumbling, "all right, all right, I was only asking."

***

"Noah! Are you there? Where are you?" Hearing nothing except hammering, Damascus cupped his hands to his mouth and yelled again. "Noah? Noah?"

A faint voice came from somewhere inside the almost complete boat, somewhere deep in the bottom of the tremendous structure, nearly as big as an aircraft carrier, a huge monstrosity. "Come down here. I can't come up right now. Lining the hull with bitumen," came the muffled cry.

"I'm coming," answered Damascus as he carefully picked his way through the timber planks, some laying loose, others nailed (wooden nails of course) in place. He descended a long ladder down to the bottom of the boat and there was Noah, filthy with bitumen all over him, applying it to the cracks between the boards of the hull. It was hot and steamy. A dreadful place, like Hell, thought Damascus.

Noah put down the wooden bucket of pitch, and said, obviously annoyed, "well, what do you want this time?"

Damascus stepped carefully off the ladder and stood in the one spot he could find that was not covered in tar. "Just need a clarification. You said two of everything. Do they have to be perfect couples?"

"There is no such thing as a perfect couple, ever since Adam and Eve. You should know that," growled Noah.

"By couple you mean…?"

"Don't you know anything? Male and female, of course. What else is there?"

Of course, Noah could not possibly know what we know today, that there are at least six variations on the idea of coupling. So he should have accepted six by six instead of two by two species representations.

Damascus bowed his head. "I'm sorry, Noah. I will have my scribe look for the closest to perfect couples he can find. Male and female. It's just that I thought…"

Noah interrupted him impatiently. "It's not your job to think. It is your job to find and count what you have been told to do. Now, off you go, and don't come back until you have your selections all lined up and ready to board."

Damascus bowed his head even more. "I apologize, sir, great one…"

"And none of that great business. You think I'm God or something? Don't be so blasphemous, or I will not allow you to join us on the boat when we set sail."

Damascus retreated, but could not help asking one more question. "Noah? May I ask, when is the flood coming? How much time do I have?"

Noah took a large handful of bitumen and splashed it on the boards of the hull. "It will be ready when you have them all lined up, and not before. The flood will come only after we have loaded the boat. Stop your worrying. It's my job to worry. Yours to get the species all lined up. Now get out of here and do your job."

Damascus retreated up the ladder, thoroughly confused. He had received no real answers to any of his questions. But at least if something went wrong, he could blame it on Noah. He came away from Noah feeling humbled, actually worse than that. He feared Noah's wrath, and resented that such a bully was so close to God. It did not seem fair to him. But, a job was a job, and he was prepared to put up with the abuse if it meant that he was assured to have a spot in the ark, along with his extended family. They would be the only humans on the boat.

And so the years went by, who knows how many. Noah was supposed to have lived for some 950 years, so you can imagine the challenges Damascus faced ferreting out and lining up his couples, supervising his scribe, recording every species and its couples, lining them up. Then there was the super-human challenge of keeping the couples all in line, well fed so they would not start eating each other, entertained and engaged. All in all, the species behaved themselves. After all, they were promised a spot on the ark, all the rest of their species doomed to drown in the coming flood.

Unfortunately, there was just one problem. A species, just a single, not a couple, showed up and insisted to the scribe that it must be included. The scribe looked it up and down. "Can't you read?" he asked impatiently, The sign says Couples Only, No Exceptions."

"What?" asked the single again, 'read'? What's that?"

"No wonder Noah only wants couples," thought the scribe to himself, "if singles are all as ignorant as this one, the world would be better off if they went down with the flood."

The scribe repeated, "you have to be a perfect couple," said the scribe, "step aside" and he scratched away at his enormously long scroll of papyrus.

The single species refused to budge. "I am a perfect couple," it said.

"You can't be," said the scribe looking up and around. "There's only one of you."

"I should be at the head of the line," complained the single. "I'm super special. There's nothing like me anywhere."

"I'm not surprised," mumbled the scribe, writing away. "In any case, even if the boss let you in, you'd have to be at the back of the line. No pushing in allowed. You have to wait your turn."

The single stood (it had legs, body and arms, looked suspiciously like a human) and refused to move. "I demand to see your supervisor," it ordered.

"He's busy counting the couples right now. Has to have the count by sundown, and ready to board at dawn tomorrow."

The single grabbed the scribe's stylus and threw it away. "I demand to see your supervisor!" it yelled, hands on hips, a most threatening manner.

The scribe stood up and stepped back, frightened. "All right! All right!" But I can tell you it will be of no use. He's around the other side of the boat. But don't blame me if you don't come back."

The single pushed his way past the scribe who fell back on the rock he usually sat on, and the first couple (foxes) kindly retrieved his stylus for him.

The single hurried around the side of the boat, an immense construction, walking towards where he heard hammering.

"Hey, are you the boss around here?" it called.

Noah continued hammering. He was putting up a welcome sign on which were carved ten principles for behaving on the boat.

"Are you deaf or something?" yelled the single. "Haven't

you got any manners? Answer me when I call you."

Noah had certainly heard this grossly indecent individual. He continued hammering.

The single impatiently ran up to Noah and grabbed the hammer just as Noah's arm was at the top of its swing. But Noah, a very strong man if ever there was one, his tough muscles well formed from the years of building the ark, easily shook the single off and swung the hammer so that it just grazed the chin of his assailant. The single fell back, and found itself sprawled on the rocky ground, trying to push itself up on its elbows.

"This is species abuse!" cried the single in a pathetically thin voice.

Noah at first ignored the single and turned his back, but then thought better of it. The individual was clearly an unsavory type and should not be trusted.

"Who are you and why have you jumped the line? And why are you not a couple?" asked Noah, swinging his hammer to and fro.

"Because," said the single, "I am a couple, but my other is inside me. I am really two. Actually, more than two, potentially."

"You speak gibberish," said Noah. "Get away and be damned! I'm surprised you even made it this far. You can't get on the ark unless you have been checked in by Damascus. And since you are clearly not a couple, you are not welcome here."

"You mean I'm doomed?" asked the single, now contrite, starting to sob.

"I wouldn't put it that way. But yes, you're doomed, both of you, if what you say is true."

"But have you no pity? Mercy even?" cried the single.

"I do," replied Noah, "but such decisions are up to God."

"Then can't you at least ask Him?"

"No, I can't. I've only been able to speak to Him a couple of times in a few hundred years. Anyway, He speaks to me. I don't get to speak to Him. Now get out of here, and let me get back to my work that will save all of humanity and animality."

Noah returned to his hammering and the single, crushed, retreated. He would have to find another way. So he went back and as he turned the corner at the bow of the boat he ran into Damascus.

"Oops, sorry" said the single.

"What are you doing here? Only couples should be behind the boat. Who gave you permission?"

"I don't need permission. I'm special," answered the single.

"Couples are special, singles are not," said Damascus impatiently.

"And I suppose you're a couple?" asked the single, sarcastically.

"My wife and I. Of course we are," answered Damascus.

"So where is she, then?" asked the single cheekily.

"None of your business. Anyway she's with our children."

"And they are all couples?" persisted the single.

Damascus looked him up and down. "Who are you, anyway?" asked Damascus, "why should I waste my time talking to you? Get away from here, go back to where you came from."

"I will not leave. I insist I have a right to get on the boat. Just because I'm special, different that is. I am a couple in myself. There's nothing else I can tell you."

"That doesn't give you the right. The rules are the rules, and they're made by God."

"But I have a right."

"Says who? I'm the boss here, and I say get to the back of the line where you belong."

The single now became very cross. "I have every right. I'm a human. I have every right."

"You can't be human, because if you were there would be two of you."

"There are."

"I see only a single. Where's your other? How can you procreate if you have no other?"

The single looked away. There was no answer to this. Damascus continued, seeing that he now had the upper hand in this silly argument. "I'll tell you what."

"Yes?" asked the single full of hope.

"Find a partner, and when there's two of you, I'll let you join the line."

"But I am two, even possibly more."

"Let's not start that again. You are obviously one, otherwise you would be two. And Noah said that no hermaphrodites were allowed. Now go!"

The single reluctantly withdrew and slouched towards the end of the line, though it snaked away to the horizon, where the end was, maybe.

***

"All aboard!" called Noah. He stepped back to peruse his sign with great satisfaction. The sign said in large letters:

NO COPULATION ALLOWED ON DECK
COUPLES MUST STAY TOGETHER
NO CROSS-SPECIES INTERMINGLING
HUMANS MUST NOT ENTER ANIMAL QUARTERS
SINGLES WILL BE THROWN OVERBOARD

"Don't all rush at once, now!" called Damascus, "keep in line, there's room for everyone." At that moment, he felt a small drop of rain. He looked towards the horizon. How on earth would all these couples fit? Damascus and the scribe stood at the entrance, making sure that all the couples were perfect couples, the scribe checking each one off as they entered. But then out of nowhere, the single appeared tugging at the scribe's elbow, jostling to the front of the line.

"I'm back, and we are a perfect couple" announced the single with much satisfaction, almost cocky.

The single had found a mate, who looked like it had come from the ice age, some kind of prehistoric thing, maybe a human. Now the rain came down in torrents. Damascus squinted through the rain at the single and its partner and pointed in the distance, "then get to the back of the line and wait your turn," he ordered. They were hardly visible through the torrents of rain, accompanied now by frightening thunder.

"But I was here before a lot of the others," whined the single, "it's not fair."

"Go to the back of the line," ordered Damascus once again, with a very tired sigh. "You may be different, but that doesn't make you special. Go to the back of the line and wait your turn."

***

As the end of the line appeared, the scribe, exhausted, but still checking off the passengers, hardly noticed the unpalatable couple shimmering through the rain that poured into his eyes and down his face. He was overjoyed that it was the last couple. Too tired to bother questioning them, he simply entered into the ship's manifest, "couple, species unknown." Damascus was so tired he fell asleep, and unbeknownst to him, the scribe with the assistance of the last couple dragged him on to the boat just as it broke away from its mooring.

Now, God sent great flashes of lightning to indicate that the voyage was beginning. And the ship sailed to who knows where, and to this day has never been found. But we know that it must have survived because couples abound everywhere and in every species all over the world. And the singles, who, having remained silent for thousands of years, have at last come forward and pleaded for their recognition as something special, and continue to demand that they be placed at the head of the line rather than relegated to the end. But as humans have developed the wonderful system of democratic government, there is no line with a front or an end. There is simply a mass within which everyone must find a place—of course, an impossibility.

e.

9. THE ZOO OF ENLIGHTENMENT

In the magnificent Museum of Old and New Art, in Hobart Tasmania, there was once an exhibit composed of a middle aged man, cropped hair, naked to the waist, sitting upright on a chair, motionless, only the image to behold, enhanced by various tattoos on chest and arms. That was it. The man did nothing. Just sat staring blankly ahead. Visitors gawked at this unexpected sight. It was a fad in zoos many years ago to exhibit a human behind bars, going about his daily business for people to stare at, just as they might stare at other animal species in the zoo. It was in the early days of the second enlightenment (late 20th century) that made people in the west accept the idea that the world should not be centered on humans as something special, that all species were equal, that therefore animals should be treated as humans, and if that were not possible, humans treated like animals. That was the small, if not a little confused message in those days. Of course, some eastern religions had long recognized this, much to the criticism by the west, the worship of cows as sacred, for example in parts of India. This enlightened view of life expressed itself in the west in many ways, the most obvious, by the rise of the vegetarians and their more extreme relatives the vegans. In the 21st century, the second enlightenment continues to flourish, traditional boundaries between species now blurred, and has expanded its influence among the intelligentsia and their handmaidens the media, to eradicate the traditional boundaries between genders and their respective intercourses. We look forward to the new forms of art that will be created and discovered during the second enlightenment.

Such is the modern zoo established recently in California, by far the most progressive state of the United States of America, indeed, the progressive leader of the rest of the world, especially the Twitter world. It therefore comes as little surprise that San Francisco, with money donated by the dark knights behind Google, Twitter, Facebook and other beacons of 21st century enlightenment, has torn down its old zoo completely and established it anew on the island where Alcatraz, the infamous prison, once stood. This zoo is like no other. It has no walls or bars except the wall that encircles its entire perimeter. Nor is it free range, although some might insist that it really is. But the popular free range zoos only allow certain animals to roam their paddocks and fields. They do not allow a free for all—the classic animal kingdom if you like, to range at will. In those zoos, lions and tigers are well fed, so they have no need to eat other animals that roam the zoo.

Think of any animal species. It is there in the Alcatraz zoo. You may not see it, depending on where you roam. That's right, not only do the animals roam, so do the humans, visitors or specimens. That is why there are many large signs that warn visitors against being eaten. The zookeepers do not feed the animals. The island is refreshed in such a way that the animals feast on each other and on whatever the perfectly reproduced "jungle" provides. So if humans are silly enough to offer themselves up to the animal predators, so be it. The zoo has only been open for two months, and so far, there has been no formal complaint laid concerning any ingestion of a human. It is true that one elephant was attacked by a pride of tigers, and every last morsel eaten by tigers, dingoes, and the like. There were no public complaints. So why should there be any if it happened to be a human? A human is no more special than an elephant. Or an ant, for that matter (so the extremists say).

Visitors to the old Alcatraz island, when the prison was still in its pristine, ugly condition, may complain that a great icon of America's criminal history has been destroyed. The builders have retained two of the original cell blocks, though they have been refurbished to provide the proper physical and cultural environment for visitors and specimens alike. Cell block one is what might be called the justice block—where the unique ability of human species to punish each other is on display (more about this exciting exhibit shortly). The second cell block is reserved for overnight and extended stays of animals and humans upon their request. That block is closed to the public once it has reached full capacity. Some have called this the animal brothel. For the moment only two species, humans and monkeys are permitted in that experimental cell block. This does not mean that other species are discriminated against. Simply we must take small steps in our great progressive agenda. But be assured for those of you who doubt us: we are committed to breaking down the boundaries of all species. To keep species separate, in our considered opinion, is tantamount to racism, the higher form of which is speciesism.

One more important point. Animals of all species do not carry weapons, though there are rare species (monkeys for example) that have been known to pick up a big stick and hit someone with it. We do allow that level of tool acquisition and use by any animals or humans that are capable of it. However, we do not allow the carrying of any other weapons, whether guns, arrows, or spears. Sharp sticks and stones are permitted. So is using stones as projectiles.

It is quite understandable if you are already thinking that this is a plan for disaster. Of course, being killed and eaten is a disaster for the one killed. And you may also be thinking that the odds for survival in our real life zoo are very much in favor of the "lion king." That remains to be seen. Besides, we object to the imperialist tone of that expression. America was established to get rid of the tyranny of a king. That was a result of the first enlightenment. This is a new age. Further, it has a genderist connotation. We think of all species as on a level playing field. All species are born equal. None is assumed to be greater than the other. All species matter. There is no better example of our commitment to this progressive idea than the cell block two exhibit, as we will shortly see.

Cell block one, the justice block, is not really a cell block. We retained only a few of the originals cells of the block (Al Capone's and the Birdman's for example), since we all know now that the major form of justice produced by the 18th century so-called enlightenment was prison, of which Alcatraz, one of its many monstrosities, is a shining example. The remaining cells were demolished to make way for the construction of the gaming room where we have perfected a justice system that eradicates all bias and systemic speciesism from the justice system. It is the opposite to enlightenment justice in which there is a finite set of crimes defined in language that only lawyers understand, presided over by judges whose fallibility is well known, and lawyers make much money off the backs of their clients, whether offenders or victims. Instead, we have erased the entire notion of offender and victim. We consider all persons, actually all species, capable of crimes, or we prefer to call them accidents or simply events that must be punished. What these events are it is unnecessary to define or even identify. In fact, of course, everyone knows that you cannot punish an event. You can only punish a person, or should I say, one of a species. Or, more precisely, one must have an object to punish. For example, kicking one's dog is an act that, in the old world, might be punishable. But again, one cannot punish the act, only the individual who did it.

Our solution to this unnecessarily complicated problem of who should be punished and what for, is simple. It eradicates completely any possibility of injustice or bias. We leave it to chance. Hence our gaming room on Alcatraz. Visitors to our zoo must sign the waiver agreement that they will abide by all rules and restrictions of the zoo, and that they enter the game room at their own risk and choice. When they enter, they receive a number and when the room is full to capacity, we literally spin the wheel and the first number up identifies the first receiver of justice. In the outside world we know that about one person every ten minutes commits some kind of crime. Thus, we spin the wheel every ten minutes. If your number comes up you step into the pain infliction machine and are subjected to a brief, but very painful, electric shock to the buttocks. The shock is administered by whatever species happens to step on one of the large levers that are hidden about the zoo, including outside the game room. Thus, the randomly chosen justice recipient may be punished by an unknown species, and that punisher may even be ignorant of its role in punishing. There are many difficulties with administering this justice and we have much to do to make sure that it cannot be tampered with. Our aim is to produce truly pure justice that is incorruptible, applicable to all regardless of their species. The misleading portrayals invented by the corrupt 18th century enlightenment officials of "lady justice" blindfolded holding the scales of justice in one hand, has always been a lie. Our justice is pure, simple, and incorruptible. In cell block one you not only see justice administered, but you also have the chance to participate, if you are lucky.

Pleas of "innocence" by the way are never accepted. Our justification for this rigid rule is the famous and prescient observation made by the only great mind of the old enlightenment, Franz Kafka, whom we hold in great awe. He wrote in his wonderful story *The Penal Colony*: "Guilt is never to be doubted." It is inscribed above the entrance to the justice room. The idea was born in the old enlightenment. We have put it into practice.

Now for cell block two. Be warned. To some, what follows may be stressful, and may cause sleepless nights. However, we do not provide prurient descriptions of the experiences in cell block two. Here, we provide only a general sketch of what happens, or may happen. One cannot for sure predict exactly what trysts will arise. It depends on many factors, the time of day, when a particular species has eaten, the actual physiological and structural make-up of the species, if you see what I mean. Inter-species intercourse may not be physically possible, though if you have watched birds at it, it is a marvel that they reproduce. The same with a large dog and a tiny dog. On the other hand species that are roughly the same size such as a horse and a donkey, are able to cross, though the outcomes are sometimes surprising. If you buy the premium ticket, you will have the opportunity to experiment yourself. We have had some customers who have a fantasy of being able to fly. At least, would like to have children who could live out that fantasy. Yes, that's right. The second enlightenment does not accept many of the old supposed adages, such as "pigs can't fly." One day, the interactive experiences possible in cell block two may show just how wrong that assertion is.

We have retained the division into cells in this and cell block one. Generally, we have knocked out the walls between every other cell to make them larger, and we have kept the bars, and the locks on the doors. We have found this necessary because, as you may know, some species can be aggressive at times, in fact some, such as certain grasshoppers, will eat their partner after sex. There is also the constant fear—I hesitate to use that word—as generally we do not encourage fear except when it is born into certain species. Some species live in fear most of the time, such as grown deer and most humans, though their babies have no such fear, and for their own good must be taught it.

In any case, we keep a selection of species in each cell, having assessed their condition or receptivity, the stage in their reproductive cycle, and so on. We rotate these different species through the cell block, and allow free cellular interaction with our human clients according to their (plural) wishes. Human clients must sign a consent form, indemnifying us from damages, and also identifying next of kin so that should something happen, the species becomes pregnant or dies for example, these outcomes may be transferred according to the client's wishes.

Some of the cells that visitors may select have options for darkening the cell, even making it pitch black. This means generally that visitors who come simply to look, rather than to take advantage of our interactive experiences, may not see what they hope to see. We do provide night vision goggles, but in environments of total darkness that some species live, that may be impossible. However, overnight and even week or month sojourns may be allowed depending on the species.

Although we have not been operating long enough to see the production of cross-progeny, we do anticipate that this will be a popular and natural outcome of our real life zoological experiences. We are working on developing a best practices schedule for those who parent such progeny, and, depending upon the assessment by our highly experienced social workers, we will come to an arrangement with the parents whether a home stay is recommended, or whether the cross progeny should remain here in the zoo.

No doubt you are already imagining all kinds of horrific scenes in which one species devours—in every sense of that word—its partner or progeny. Once again, we remind you that this is a real life interactive zoo. All behaviors that occur in the wild (a nasty racist word) are possible and indeed encouraged in this zoo. Its outcomes are explored and demonstrated in cell block one.

***

A modern zoo would not be complete without a performance arena, which is what we made from the old exercise yard of Alcatraz, famous for its image of the criminals walking around and around the yard, single file in a circle, as imagined in many drawings and photoshopped photographs. But even the smallest of animal zoos have always included in their exhibits, a performance section where animals of a wide variety are "civilized" by being taught to do many wondrous tricks by the masters, the humans. In the performances we offer, we try to level the playing field as far as it is possible, though keeping an eye out for acts that animals can do and humans cannot. The most well-known of these is the seal balancing a beach ball on its nose. How many humans can do that? It turns out quite a few, with the right training. Our "ringmaster" as we call our chief training executive will show you how it's done (additional charge for admission to the performances). However, we do like to keep the performances as part of our overall interactive approach, so the trainer will allow members of the audience to select the method of training, (reinforcement with rewards, or punishment with painful electric shock). Of course, the majority of the audience favors the electric shock schedule. They say electric shock is more "humane" (a species-ist word if ever there was one, certainly an insult to the animals including those that claim humanity), because it does not draw blood of even leave much of a mark on the body, or more correctly the exo- or intro-skeleton, thorax, head, abdomen, legs arms or antennae.

As an aside, you may have taken offense at our use of the word "ringmaster" which on first hearing sounds prejudiced, certainly the nasty connotation of master and slave. The word comes, of course, from the now defunct circuses that treated their animals badly, though we insist, not as bad as regular zoos, since circuses did have humans perform as clowns and sometimes as acrobats or contortionists, performing alongside their equals, elephants, tigers, lions etcetera.

Here is a brief listing of the performing species, though it changes constantly, depending on what species are available and at what stage of regeneration they have reached. However, we do apologize for not including microorganisms in our displays or performances. Be assured that this is among our forthcoming exhibits, when we have obtained the necessary funding to set up micro-view facilities. And to be honest, the extremists on equality are putting great pressure on us to consider microorganisms as part of the universal species list, so they argue that micro-organisms should have the same rights as larger species. Just because they are small, does not mean they have fewer rights. They have the same right to life as any other species or class of species. Obviously there are very serious implications of this expansive view of universal rights and these are still being worked out. For the moment, our leading science ethicists do not agree that microorganisms, especially those that may cause widespread death and destruction such as a pandemic, should be treated just like any other form of life which we hold precious. For the moment, they advocate keeping alive only a few samples of such species (one never knows whether they may turn out to be a force for the good), and the rest should be euthanized.

The performances that may be seen in our interactive arena are:

- Applying electric shock, teaching a bull terrier to bite a black person's hand and lick a white person's hand (and vice-versa).
- Applying electric shock to train a human to lick the paw of a dog, and to bite the hand of a monkey.
- Using a sharp prodding instrument, such as used by

Indian elephant trainers, to teach an elephant to balance on one leg. Do the same with a person except require the balance on an inflated beach ball.

- Have humans imitate copulation techniques from a group of macaques, and explore inter-species mating.
- Have humans fight bare handed with selections of species that are upright walkers or runners, such as the gorilla and monkey species, kangaroos, and bears.

We provide this list merely as suggestions and to give the flavor of what to expect. Remember, we are entering the second enlightenment. Anything is possible. We encourage you to send us suggestions for species performances, now that we have opened your minds to these fascinating possibilities.

It was the performance arena that forced us to face up to the biggest taboo of the last many centuries that culminated in the first enlightenment, and raised humans up to a very high pedestal. The second enlightenment, while much has been achieved in breaking down decrepit taboos and old fashioned practices that have no cultural value, or that discriminate with or without intent, has forced us at the Zoo of Enlightenment to face up to the one immovable taboo that has remained unquestioned in civilizations everywhere. This is the taboo of cannibalism. Yes, there have been unique occurrences when cannibalism was forced on people marooned on an island, or lost in a desert, or some other extenuating circumstance. Though as evidence of the depth of this taboo, many of those caught in those unusual situations chose to die before giving in to eating another of their species. Once we saw the insidious speciesism hiding within the expression "Animal Kingdom" as we noted earlier, we realized that we had to confront it.

Generally speaking, the supposed hierarchy of the animal kingdom puts those at its top (lions, tigers etc. plus humans) of the "food chain" as it is called, essentially an arbitrary ordering of those who live off the lives of those beneath them. This is hardly in line with the idea of species equality engendered by the second enlightenment. Besides, there is also the question of population control.

But we are getting ahead of ourselves.

As an intermediate step towards full species equality, we offer a full funeral service to our premium customers who can have themselves of their loved ones who pass away returned to the "animal kingdom" and thus fed to the lions and other meat-eating species. There are certain formal requirements for those offering their bodies, and our brochure outlines all of these. For example, whether you want the bones to be crushed and turned into fertilizer, pecked clean by vultures and other meat eating birds or animals, and so on. Our aim is always to assist you in returning your loved ones to the earth from whence they came. This is, however, an interim step. By the way, we will offer a wide choice of animals for feasting, and it is part of our ten year plan to add a shark pool on the west side of the island where loved ones can be fed to the sharks.

We look forward to breaking down the greatest taboo of all that has masqueraded as the jewel of civilization, that of cannibalism, exploited by the imperialists of the first enlightenment to justify their colonization of so-called primitive peoples who routinely practiced it. As part of our reparations to those "savages" we will accept applications from those whose natural pre-imperialist societies were destroyed, to join the "animal kingdom" in the arena and stalk volunteer white supremacists and feast upon them. Our ultimate aim, of course, is to have all peoples, regardless of race or color, to feast on each other, to live in "wild" equality. We acknowledge that this is maybe an unreachable goal, but following the Paris accord on climate change, we believe in setting up such goals to spur societies on, to make the commitment of reparations and repair the damage done to the world by 18th century enlightenment and before. By the year 2050 we will achieve zero inequality..

10. THE SLOUGH OF
DECENCY

A pilgrim journeys to the University of the Chosen

Grace, exhausted, sore and confused, was pushed into a holding cell whereupon she collapsed on the floor. The crowd of young people milled around her. They too were sore and hurt. They were her fellow protesters and they had just been deposited here after the violent confrontation they had against police in front of Washington's Capitol. Someone lifted her up and placed her on a bunk, where she lay, in a swoon, a dream emerging from her mouth as if she were a character in a comic book. She tried to sit up, but felt an unbearable weight on her shoulders, and fell back. And then, under the weight of many hands, strange cold hands, her dream took off, a journey, one full of hope, to who knows where it would take her. But the weight on her shoulders held her back.

She was accepted into the University of the Chosen and the day had come for her to leave her Celestial Suburb and say good-bye to her parents, Pride and Doting Dolittle. They called to her in unison: "Take care our little white girl, take care! Drive carefully!" Grace opened the door of her new electric car that she had Christened "Savior," but the weight on her shoulders stopped her from entering. She brushed and slapped at her

115

shoulders, but the more she did so the heavier the weight. Then suddenly, the weight on her shoulders revealed itself. It was a wizened little monkey-looking thing as fat as it was tall, skinny hairy legs which it tightened around Grace's neck.

"Let me in and I will show you the way," said the disgusting smelling monkey.

"Who, who are you?" asked Grace, shaking in fear.

"Just call me Luke," answered the monkey, with a devilish grin.

What a strange name! She had never heard it before. In any case, Grace complied without thinking any more about it. She just had to get to university, it was all she had thought about for the past year. She said the magic words, "Phi Beta Kappa," the car door opened, the weight on her shoulders lifted, and she slid into the seat, only to find Luke sitting at the steering wheel.

"I'll drive. I know where to go. University of the Chosen, wasn't it?" Luke growled.

What else could Grace do but sit back and accept? But no sooner had she done so than they turned a corner and were suddenly in a suburb of the Lost. Or that was what she guessed, having heard of such a suburb, but had never been in one before.

"Don't worry. These are all my friends," said Luke.

"All of them?" Grace wished she had as many friends.

"All of them."

The car stopped at a corner where Grace pointed to a group of young African Americans chatting and laughing.

"You shouldn't use that word, you know," said Luke.

"What word?" asked Grace, feeling a massive weight return to her shoulders.

"You called them niggers."

"I said no such thing. I didn't utter a word!"

"They don't call me Devil for nothing, you know. Now

apologize."

"I thought your name was Luke?"

"It is. Short for Lucifer, don't you like it?"

"Oh No! You're the Devil that Proud and Doting warned me about!"

"At your service."

Devil lowered the passenger side window where Grace could lean out to say her apology. "Now apologize! Go on then, say it!" he ordered.

Grace had always done what she was told. This was no exception.

"Guys, I mean you people, I'm sorry!" called Grace in a weak voice.

The group turned to her, made cat calls, called her white bitch and invited her to sleep with them.

Devil intervened. "You can't sleep with them. They're black and you're a white supremacist."

"What? I don't want to…"

"Yes you do. You're disgusting. Imagine what Pride and Doting would say if they knew that's what you want at the University of the Chosen."

"But we're not at the University of the Chosen yet, are we?"

"Not quite. But you see that guy standing on his own, all dressed so nice and his hair combed flat with a perfect part?"

"He's one of the Chosen?" asked Grace, wide-eyed.

"Now you're getting it." Devil called out. "Hey you there, blackie, get in."

The well-dressed boy or girl of the ghetto came over, as if called like a dog. Grace opened the door. "Climb in. We can all fit in the front," she said in her most friendly voice.

"Hello," he or she said. "Before I get in, you should know that I'm not what you think I am."

"She knows that," grinned Devil, as they sped off and out

of the suburb of the lost.

"I don't know," said Grace once again feeling that weight on her shoulders.

"Yes. I'm not a full African American. I'm a half-caste," said the boy or girl or whatever.

"So what?" said Grace, feeling confident, "that means nothing to me."

Devil intervened. "Careful, Grace. Careful what you say."

"My name is Algy," said the half African American with a grin.

"That's a nice name," said Grace, entranced and puzzled. "Is that what makes you so different?"

"Yes, you could say that. It stands for LG. Get it?"

Devil nudged Grace in the ribs. "Come on, say it, you know what it stands for."

"You mean LGBTQIA?" she asked nervously.

"That's about right," answered Algy with a smile that displayed his sparkling white teeth. His hand was already on her thigh.

"That's amazing. You're the first!" exclaimed Grace.

"Okay, you two. That's enough," ordered Devil. "We're there anyway. Where all the white girls are is your door, Grace. The rest go in the other door."

Grace thanked Devil and offered to pay for the ride. "No need," said the Devil. "I'll keep an account. You'll pay soon enough."

"But my car?"

"Don't worry. It will be in the Chosen carpark waiting for you."

Grace turned to look for the campus, its beautiful old porticos, carved wooden doors. But she could see hardly any of this, just the tall spires peeping out above the haze. And there before her, was a large oily looking lake that lay between her and the entrance, her door, to the University of the

Chosen. She looked for Algy who had quickly left her and disappeared into the haze. Maybe he knew of a secret way into the University. She stood there, puzzled. Between her and the dim outlines of the Chosen lay an uninviting lake, dark in color, almost as thick as black mud. The weight on her shoulders had returned, though it had slipped on to her back, like a knapsack full of stones.

She had come so far, the university almost in reach. Yet, there was no way she could get there. She dipped her toes in the lake, but pulled them out quickly. It was like a bog. She could not swim in it. The weight of Despair descended upon her, forcing her to drop down on her haunches. She wept. And in between the sobs, she looked up hoping that the haze would recede and the lake depart. Then she prayed, she knew not to whom or what. She had heard about people praying, but knew nothing of it. She had seen movies in which Muslims prayed and Buddhists chanted. Perhaps that was what she should do?

Now she lay down on the muddy grass, its coolness helping calm her small bosom. But under the weight, she heaved and sobbed, cried herself into a disturbed sleep. At which point help arrived.

Out of the gloom appeared a boatman, whistling joyfully as he rowed his kayak with gentle and rhythmic gusto. "Hey, you over there, are you one of the Chosen?"

Grace awoke. Was she having a dream within a dream? She stood and waved. The boatman was maybe an answer to her prayers? She had not asked for it. Had not asked for anything specifically. Only crying out for her wish to be granted. To get to the University of the Chosen where she knew she belonged. She waved and called out in her weak thin little girl's voice, "I'm here! I'm Grace, I want to go to Chosen University, but can't cross this awful lake! Is this the only way in?"

"My dear, this is the Slough of Decency. It is not a lake,

per se. It's a bog, which the Board of the University of the Chosen refuses to drain. They say it would disturb the natural environment. There are ways around it. But those are reserved for the special few as part of the University reparations agreement."

The boatman put out his hand. "Come, I will row you across, though you will have to take up an oar as well. It's a two person boat."

"Oh, thank you kind sir!" cried Grace, full of joy.

"It's what I'm here for, my dearest."

As soon as Grace climbed into the boat, the weight of Despair fell right off and into the Slough of Decency, which bubbled and gurgled in response.

"Hang on now!" cried the boatman. "It may be a rough crossing!"

"And what is your name, good person?" asked Grace, putting on the best air of Decency that she could.

"They call me Morality, because they say that without it, there could be no Decency."

"Then Mr. Morality, why are you in the Slough of Decency. I thought all moral people would always be Decent?"

"Well, that's the trouble. And it's why there is such a bog of Decency."

"I don't understand."

"Too many people claim morality, see it in everything and everyone, especially words," said the boatman. "You have to be really careful in what you say, and even if you are, there's always someone who can denounce you as immoral. So everyone's scared to say or do anything. There's an excess of Decency, that's what."

"An excess of Decency? What's that?"

"It's this bog. That's what it is. Each and every day the claims of Decency grow and grow and the Slough gets bigger and bigger."

"That's terrible, Mr. Morality!"

"Shhhh! Careful what you say, someone may hear you," whispered Morality, "you can't say Mister."

Grace fell silent, thinking. Then the outlines of the spires and stone porticos became much clearer, and so did her mind.

"Mr. Morality, or is it Miss, Ms. or Mrs?" she asked a little cheekily.

"I'm a lady, if that's what you're asking," answered Morality. "There are no moral men, even at your young age, you should know that."

Grace put her hand to her mouth. "What a horrible lady," she thought to herself. And at that moment, there was a sudden jolt of the boat and the boat-lady changed into the ugly monkey she recognized as Luke, the Devil. "You're not a lady, she cried, you're Devil!" She felt the weight once more on her shoulders.

"We're here," cackled Devil.

With great difficulty, Grace struggled out of the kayak. "You horrible man," she said, "all those nasty words you used. You should be ashamed of yourself!" She threw the oar that she had never used right at Devil's snarling face. He ducked, and it flew into the bog which gurgled and bubbled. And Grace felt the oily mud rising up to her knees."

"You better hurry if you want to make it to orientation!" cackled Devil.

Grace struggled, her feet feeling like stones. But she was determined. Nobody, nothing, would stop her from getting into the University of the Chosen. The weight on her shoulders pressed down, but she would not sink, not here. And with an herculean effort she pulled her feet out of her Nikes and made one unholy leap to the shore and landed with such a thump.

***

When Grace woke she found herself in a large hall, surrounded by empty mahogany chairs. The weight was no longer on her shoulders. She looked around but saw no one. Yet she felt that she was not alone. She brushed at her shoulders, afraid that Devil was sitting there once more. But it was not. She looked up and was dazzled by the high ceiling that seemed to reach to the heavens, decorated in gold leaf. And there were flying humans, they had wings, painted, or were they moving? She shook her head and cried, "where am I?"

One of the flying humans descended from the ceiling, her, or its, massive butterfly wings fluttering, causing Grace's hair to flutter in the cold breeze. "Who are you?" asked Grace, frightened that it would be Devil yet again.

"I am your Archangel," sang the flying human or whatever it was. "I am here to guide you on your journey."

"But I thought my journey was over. Have I not arrived at the University of the Chosen?" asked Grace in her quivering little voice, feeling a little like Alice in Wonderland.

"You are almost there, my dearest. But you must, before entering, wash your feet clean of the mud you have brought with you from the Slough of Decency."

"Oh dear, I'm so sorry. I apologize for all the bad words I have said," cried Grace putting her hand to her mouth.

"And what of those you have not spoken?" asked the Archangel with a frown.

"But, but I can't stop words coming into my head," pleaded Grace. They're not bad unless I say them, are they?"

"Bad thoughts are evil thoughts just the same, when you are at the University of the Chosen. Surely you knew that before coming here? It was written very clearly in the brochure for new students, it's right there in the mission statement. Let me show you."

Archangel fluttered her wings and pulled out from under her, or its, flowing white silky robes a scroll that said:

"The University of the Chosen is dedicated to excellence in education and considers free speech that expresses the mission of the university to be the right and duty of every Chosen student. Excellence is demanded at all times and in all things, and our diversity-inspired curriculum reflects that dedication."

"That doesn't say anything about bad thoughts," said Grace nervously.

"You have not read the footnote," replied Archangel.

Grace strained to read the footnote. It stated: "Speech is defined as any word spoken or not verbalized, hinted at, or conveyed by any sign or action, or kept secret and not shared with others."

"You see, my dear?" said the Archangel with an exagg-erated, loving smile.

"Oh dear! I didn't read the footnote. Doting and Pride I am sure did not either."

"Never mind, Grace. We can fix that up easily. After all, that is why the University of the Chosen has a crash orientation course for every new student. Follow me through the wicket gate at the end of this room, this is called the mahogany room by the way, and the orientation room is called the blue and gold room."

"Those are the colors of the University!" observed Grace, excitedly.

"That's right," beamed Archangel, "and soon you will be wearing them!"

"I am so happy!" chirped Grace, feeling like Dorothy in the Wizard of Oz. She felt herself scooped up in Archangel's arms, transported aloft, then swooped down straight through the wicket gate. And there, resplendent in the room of blue and gold she found herself standing before a crowd of Chosen students all talking excitedly.

***

Grace stirred on her bunk. Her eyes fluttered a little and through the blur she saw the rest of her fellow demonstrators milling about in the holding cell. Some banged on the bars, chanting "Free-dom! Free-dom!" But Grace was too overcome by exhaustion and confusion, it was easier to close her eyes and return to her dream, if that is what it was.

The crowd of Chosen students gathered around her. Archangel had departed to the heavens. She found herself kneeling, hands clasped together, head bowed. The Chosen began to chant.

"Inno-*cent* or ignor-*ant*?! Inno-*cent* or ignor-*ant*?!"

Was she on trial? But this was a university. Was it not the haven of freedom?

The Dean of the Freshly Chosen stepped forward and signaled for the chanting to stop. "Silence please, fellow, I mean…"

She was interrupted with boos and hisses.

"Silence please, chosen ones!" she cried. "We have before us our newest and freshest student. She, I mean who, has overcome many challenges on the journey to this, the Chosen University, the sanctuary of excellence and freedom!"

"Inno-*cent* or ignor-*ant*?! Inno-*cent* or ignor-*ant*?!" chanted the Chosen.

The Dean raised a hand signaling silence, and the chants gradually died away. "Let me say this," she-it exclaimed. "You know the old saying, though nobody knows where it came from, 'Forgive them Lord for they know not what they do?' "

The student response was a buzz of muttering and joking. The Dean was of course a thing of authority and so should be treated as such.

"I am sure, in fact I know, that every Chosen one in this room has acted out of ignorance, especially before you were bathed in excellence at this grand institution of highest education."

Applause and cheers filled the splendid room of blue and gold, and on cue, the Chosen chanted, "Blue and gold! Blue and gold!"

The Dean looked down on Grace, still kneeling, her bare knees stinging with pain. She looked up, as though pleading. Indeed, she was pleading—pleading for admission.

The Dean raised its arms signaling another silence. The Chosen complied. It then placed its hand on Grace's head and said, "do you, Grace Dolittle solemnly swear allegiance to the University of the Chosen, so help you?"

"I do!" whispered Grace.

"Speak out, Grace. We didn't hear you," said the Dean in her or its strong voice.

"I DO!" cried Grace. "I do, I do, I do!"

The Dean then announced, with one hand still on Grace's head, the other raised aloft in a Nazi-like salute. "I hereby proclaim you innocent, and may your ignorance be left behind from whence you came!"

Deafening cries and cheers filled the great blue and gold room. The Dean continued. "Rise Grace Dolittle, once of the Celestial Suburb! Rise and become one of the Chosen!"

Grace rose, all weight was lifted from her, so much so that she floated up above the crowd of Chosen, like Saint Catherine floating above the stairs.

***(

As they say, what goes up must come down. And so it was with Grace. For that splendid moment of ecstasy, acceptance into the Chosen, wafting above the crowd of Chosen, she looked down upon them—and here's the ironic part—it caused her to feel superior. She had been Chosen. She was one them, no longer one of the deplorables of the Celestial Suburb. They were not chosen. And she heard Pride and Doting Dolittle, her mom and dad, calling out to her, their voices so distant. She called out to them, "Mom! Dad!" and then regretted it so much. But it was too late. The crowd of Chosen had heard that plaintive cry, and they yelled out as one, "She's guilty! She's guilty!"

And suddenly all the lightness that had held her aloft disappeared, her balloon had popped and she fell to earth with a terrible plop.

She awoke to see the blur of faces staring down at her. Her fellow protesters had taken a moment to ask if she was all right. She had fallen off her bunk.

Anyone here called Grace? Your father has bailed you out!" called the jailer.

11. THE IDIOT

I am the world's unluckiest person. And no, don't feel sorry for me, and no, I am not exaggerating. How else can one explain the inheritance—not my doing obviously—of two despised diseases, autism (so-called) and Huntington's disease (deadly). And no, I don't feel sorry for myself, in fact, quite the opposite. How can his be?

Why should any being like me exist at all?

Now there's the real question, the one that in fact threatens my life, worse, threatens my very existence. I'm not repeating myself. There's a big difference. My life is, at bottom, the same as yours. You're born. You die. Nothing new there. It's the lot of all beings (with some micro-biological exceptions, and maybe many more depending on how one defines "death" or "life" since some organisms appear to replicate themselves by replacing dead cells with new cells at a rapid rate so the line between death and life is arbitrary). But the most horrible situation in which I find myself in this day and age (I'm not saying what year because events come and go so quickly time is sort of irrelevant, except that I do know, and the experts have threatened me with this, that my time is limited.)

In fact my doctors have threatened to kill me if I don't do what they ask. Has your doctor ever made such a direct threat? I should think not. But you see, my doctors (so-called) are not like your doctors. My doctors are experts in precision medicine. Your usual doctors aren't precise at all. Most of their treatment is a guessing game, especially for primary care or general practitioner doctors. They try something, and if it does not work, something else, and if that doesn't work they refer you to a specialist, who does more specialized guessing.

***

Precision medicine is no longer the coming thing. It has arrived much too quickly, and one of its early victims is me, yours truly. Calling myself a victim? So I am feeling sorry for myself after all? Not in the least. I am proud of it. In fact, I flaunt my victim status as much as I can, because it is the only tool I have to stop the fast lock-step march to erase people like me from this earth.

It happened so quickly, the precision medicine I mean, not my "disabilities" (so-called). The scientists who made it all possible had been slaving away in their laboratories, publishing technical breakthroughs in *Nature* magazine, competing for Nobel prizes in medical related research. The truth of their findings was amplified by revelations of the "bad science" of Sir Francis Galton (revered and worshipped by scientists for almost a century) who chose to apply his findings of inherited human characteristics to a social and legal policy that justified the sterilization of millions of peoples deemed degenerate (that's me) or whatever, all over the "civilized" world. After all it was just like a farmer breeding cattle or selective planting to produce a higher yielding crop. Besides, the Romans killed off their disabled babies, and it was the Romans who invented a civilization that lasted for a thousand years and prepared the way to the modern civilization that we have now—one whose top priority is the health and wellness of all humans who are fortunate to live in a modern society such as ours.

Except that—and here's why I am the unluckiest human on the planet. As I said, I was born with two maladies, autism that appeared when I was a baby, and Huntington's Chorea that appeared later in my twenties. My father carried the mutated HTT gene which I had a fifty percent chance of inheriting. So much for that kind of luck. Then again, as if God were trying to make amends for the error, the form of autism I inherited revealed itself as, what everyone called under their breath, an idiot savant—I was a mathematics genius from the day I could talk (maybe before, but my parents didn't notice it then). The experts call it hypercalculia, as if by giving it a name somehow explained it. But it's more than that. My memory is infinite and lightning fast. I made a lot of money in my late teens and early twenties at card games in the Las Vegas casinos (counting cards). They banned me of course. But not until I had made enough money to take care of myself the rest of my "life" (not quite sure what to call it).

A common characteristic of my kind of autism is that we display asocial obnoxious behavior that ticks a lot of people off. They say I am aggressive, forceful, have no empathy. Fair enough, as nobody, especially after I developed Huntington's had any empathy or sympathy for me—well, the sympathy I discerned was expressed in lavish, sonorous oh how dreadful poor thing—a kind of whining expressing how sorry they are for me. None of it of course is genuine. What they are so "upset" about is that they cannot show what they really think, which is that they are very, very pleased and relieved that they do not have such a malady.

Harsh? You try being stuck in a room, unable to walk hardly at all, and if so, in a dreadful drunken-looking stagger. By the time I was in my thirties, I could barely talk, and when I did, my mouth moved in jagged contortions, my tongue flopped around inside and outside my mouth. I sounded like a hungry cow trying to talk. And spit dribbled and drooled down my chin, and my lips sprayed the spit everywhere when they went into a spasm and vibrated together as if I were shivering cold. The best I could do to make life almost bearable was to fall back on my autistic excellence. It worked for a while, but gradually I had to give it up.

The sex, that is.

***

Don't blame me! Blame the fucking genes that should have been neutralized before I was born. They had the technology to edit genomes before birth—CRISPR and the rest. Blame the pathetic weasels in Congress that wouldn't allow it. They woke up pretty soon in 2018 after Doctor He Jiankui in China edited the genomes of a pair of twins embryos —the mutation of CCR5 that prevents catching HIV. He jumped the gun, supposedly faked the patient disclosure agreement, and skipped a lot else. He was drummed out of the gene science establishment, his science criticized as shabby, and his bosses back in China faked a trial that he broke Chinese Government regulations or laws. Whatever. No outsiders were able to cover the trial. Supposedly he got three years in prison for his colossal achievement. Only then did the scientists of the West wake up, and of course, the politicians. The scientists (competitors like no other, ruthless, cunning, creative and secretive) all of them in a race for grabbing the next news headline with a new break-through in gene editing. And the politicians, of course, took both sides, while all the time making sure that money found its way into the bank accounts of the many nonprofit and for-profit corporations that were formed to exploit the wonderful discoveries.

In the meantime, I adapted my uncontrollable life to circumstance.

***

A light tap on my door, three dots, three dashes, three dots. Not especially original but it was all we needed. Anyway, I only ever had two visitors, my precision doctor and my physiotherapist. This knock combination was my physiotherapist. She came every other day, 2.00 pm precisely. Because of my malady I could not call out "come in" in any intelligible way. That was why the door was never locked. The brass handle turned, and in she came, today dressed in a very, very, tight and almost non-existent bikini, covered by a see-through veil, an old wedding veil, I'd bet. My tongue poked itself out the side of my mouth as and I tried to sit up in bed to greet her. This was, of course, physically impossible for me. My back muscles were long ago shriveled into coarse stiff meat like that of a half cooked horse leg. Instead I rolled off the bed, my arms splayed out in an effort to stop the fall, my head flopping on its neck, my chin banging on my shoulder bone. This, I was used to, as was my physiotherapist.

"Hello handsome!" she cried with a big smile, her mouth the widest of any I had known.

And before I hit the floor head first, she threw herself down and I landed like a writhing uncontrollable quadropus, my spit and dribble landing on her veil.

"Poor darling!" she said.

And then she began her therapy. Her instructions from my precision doctor were to keep me satisfied and happy, no matter what she had to do. And believe me, she did that with an enthusiasm anyone would envy.

I have lost count of the days, maybe weeks or even months that I have been receiving this therapy designed to keep me well satisfied, though I suspect my precision doctor was under orders not to let me fall into depression and commit suicide. Not that it would be easy for me to do. Lying there alone, unable to move much of the time, I had dreamed up ways to do it. Probably the most effective would be to stick my fingers or most of my hand into my throat and try to choke myself. My thinking was that once I stuck my fingers in there, I would not have the strength to pull them out.

Yet, on my better days, usually the hour or so after my

physiotherapist had delivered her therapy, I reflected on my short life, an amazing life it had been. I had won at cards (I know, I told you that already), but what I didn't tell you is that my autistic mathematics brilliance got me into Harvard, and in great demand by a lot of labs that were conducting research on genome splicing and editing. That work was all about mathematics, the necessity of not being over-awed at the colossal numbers involved. Some forty trillion human cells in each individual, DNA strings of letters, some 67 billion miles long unraveled and placed end-to-end for humans, though some 20 percent shorter than that of a mouse. The strings composed of just four letters ATGC at times obviously repeated patterns, many palindromes, and other strings seemingly random. An MIT lab that I will not name snapped me up, and I worked there, so, so happy, applying my math, the bigger the numbers the more complex the patters, the more I liked it. I was the marvel of the lab that had, at the time, some thirty researchers. I was a perfect match for science: my autistic characteristic of enjoying repetitive boring work so necessary in a scientific lab. To "normal humans" (I'm not, obviously) such repetitive work is drudgery. Not for me. It was when I was most relaxed.

The only down side, I suppose a regret, was that as part of my so-called savant-like autism I was not able to write. I could read like a wizard, and remember every page word for word. But when it came to putting findings or ideas down on paper, or typing something up, I was annoyingly unable to put the words together. The precision doctors called it dysgraphia. The result was that I was rarely listed as a coauthor in the important publications in *Nature* that all my scientific colleagues thirsted for. Resentment? No. It never entered my head. Once again, my autistic brilliance shielded me from what everyone calls ambition, and in the science field the comp-etition to become THE winner in the perpetual scientific race to discover something new. And what were they looking for? Celebrity status? Fame? I had no need of that. My autistic brilliance had already done that for me over and over.

My physio struggled to lift me up onto the bed which was, in fact, a special bed very low to the floor so that when I fell out of bed I would not hurt myself. Not that she wasn't without strength. She was well muscled. But handling my body was trying to lift a limp drunk. There was little I could do to make her task easier. She had to lift first my legs, if she could grab them and stop them from flaying about, on to the bed, then get on the bed and drag them a leg under each arm, and manage eventually to roll my butt on to the bed. That done, she let go and grabbed one of my arms in very tight hands and managed to pull the rest of me on to the bed.

These sessions lasted some three hours. And she did this every other day. Surely she must have been sick of it. But I was not. What more could one ask for, a constantly randy thirty year old. Just lying in wait, serviced every other day? That's the nice way of putting it. In fact, I was raped every day, much to my delight.

***

My precision doctor is a large stout woman. If I could talk well enough to be understood I would tell her she should have her genes analyzed and get rid of the ones that make her fat. Trouble is, in my condition I can only sort of talk with a lot of effort, hard to keep my tongue from rolling about, and I just can't convey to her or others the nuances that are the main part of speech, effected by tiny movements of the tongue to cause a sound to waver in a particular way, slight movements of the lips—oh how I miss being able to move them into snarls or smiles, or something in between. And my lips move in unison (sorry, they used to move) with my cheeks, and the slight drop of my chin, or poking it forward. You know what I'm talking about, don't you? It's all the finer movements that make up facial expression, that convey directly what's in my mind. Of course, assuming the person or persons I am talking to have either the empathy or skill to listen to me. But then again, in my opinion most persons do not have the patience to listen to ordinary people talking to them, so why would they make the extra effort to listen to me?

Nevertheless it's a good thing that my precision doctor is a stout and strong woman, otherwise she could not cope with me in my uncontrollable state, arms and legs thrashing about, loud tiger-like growls as I try to speak. Yet, kudos to her. She seems to be able to understand what I am saying, the words buried in the growls and lately screams that my slobbering mouth exudes, and my futile attempts to convey their meaning with my hands and arms. Truly useless gesticulations. She does, however, treat me like some kind of insect, a spider maybe. Being a scientist she is fascinated by my strangeness. Yet being a scientist, she lacks empathy, and certainly not one bit of sympathy for my conditions. I am a specimen to her. That's all. I have tried to tell my parents that on the very rare occasions they have visited me in my present condition, stuck in a room, a windowless cell, though large with much technological gear, humming machines, once huge and mighty, now tiny and super mighty. Of all of that I was once a part and loved it. The lab at MIT. Those were the days. Power, devotion, and, when we discovered a new technique, new splicing of particular genes, nothing less than ecstasy. Little did we, or at least I, know what we were really doing. We were changing the world, or more accurately, innocently providing the tools that would allow those who lusted for power (politicians, of course, who else?) to change the world.

But enough. I hear a scraping at my door. Yes, I am not deaf yet, and I can see not too badly, though it will not be long before those senses decline, or become uncontrollable, which might be worse. The door will open immediately and my PD

(Precision Doctor) will enter. The door is never locked (yes, I repeat myself). I am incapable of getting to the door, let alone turning a door knob. And my PD simply walks in whenever she likes, no knock.

She stands just inside the door, her broad shoulders held back, as though she were a captain of the guards, then her hands on her hips, head well back, her chin up. She's a well-kept person in her fifties. Few wrinkles, though a face that has a pinkish gray complexion, strands of gray in her hair that is coifed up into deep sea-like waves that break on to her shoulders.

"And how are we this morning?" she says, "have a nice visit from your physio yesterday?"

I grumble and try to roll way on the bed to avoid facing her. But my body has its own design and instead rolls the other direction, arms and legs shaking and kicking, and I roll off the bed and on to the floor. "UUUck!" I manage to blurt. She knows what I am trying to say.

"Now. Now. Enough of that. Keep it for your physio," growls my PD.

I just stay where I am, trying to keep still, which is impossible. She leans down and with an almighty grunt, grabs my shoulders and pulls me up, almost throws me back on my bed.

"I have some good news and some bad news," she says.

I am now lying on my back, legs and arms shaking and shivering. I try to look at her. Can't move my head where I want. But my eyes still move in her direction. She continues as though I have answered her.

"You want the bad news first? Yes, I thought so. Best to get it out of the way. "Your parents will be here shortly. We have allowed them to visit you today, because tomorrow they will be de-gendered per article 623.41 US Penal Code, and New York State penal codes 5X31.289."

This was ridiculous and outrageous, I am sure anyone

would agree. My parents were the same age probably as my PD. And besides, I had nothing against them. It was not their fault I was born with the genes I have. I mean, it was Nature, wasn't it? I mean, they inherited their genes from their parents so why not blame their parents? And their parents' parents?"

Of course, I could not say any of this to my stout PD. But I did frown as much as I could to convey my displeasure. Of course, my PD chose to misunderstand my response.

"I know," she said also with a frown, but her thin lips holding back a slight smile.

"Waaaawaaaaawuuuun!" I cried. I hope you guessed it. I was telling her that it was unjust because only one of them carried the Huntington gene (dear old dad), and it was just bad luck that I got it.

Correction. Being an experienced gambler and card counter, I do not believe luck plays a part at all. Besides, criminalizing people for (1) having and (2) transmitting a bad gene was nothing to do with luck. It was sheer political power having its way. And when you think about it, this is a dreadful observation. Because the "way" that politicians took was supported by the findings of science. Is that not so? And my PD would be first to acknowledge this, though her acquiescence would be shrouded within all kinds of philosophical-come-ethical standards of her profession that were hammered out in many special committees composed of bioethicists, chemists, gene splicers, bioengineers, molecular biologists, physicists and many more.

At just the right time, there was a faint knock at my door. Of course, it would be my parents. They would be too overwhelmed by the circumstances to just barge in like my PD does. My door knob turned and in they walked.

My parents entered, hand in hand—at their age, really? PD stood where she was, looking straight at me. No doubt that guilt and lots of it sat heavily on her shoulders.

"YouaaahhhFurrrghk!" I screamed.

My parents timidly stopped just inside the door as it quietly closed behind them. My PD knew exactly what I was saying. I was telling her that she was a fucking bitch and it was her fault that she had let my parents slip past her when they originally consulted her concerning my genome—that is, before I was born, when I was, essentially a cell. I know how it happened. They were both professors, mother in literature, father in history. They insisted that there was no need for them to go through the usual screening of embryo or each of their genomes. They were obviously a good match, both professors, no history of any genetic disease in either of them or their ancestors. In fact they had cunningly sent swabs of saliva that was not theirs, but was swiped from a couple of half empty coffee cups in the University Cafeteria. They had both figured that if only one of them had the faulty gene, there was a reasonable 50-50 chance that I would not be born with it.

And so it seemed. They ignored my autism, which was not as far as they could tell a result of any genetic ancestry. In fact, my brilliance at mathematics overawed them and they boasted of my brilliance to whoever would listen. They were professors after all. Why would not their child be brilliant?

It was only with the onset of Huntingdon's that they began to realize that they had made a colossal mistake. They had, ironically, gambled with my life.

You may have been wondering why I referred to them as "my parents." No "Mom and Dad." I never felt close to them. I blamed it on my autism. In fact, I never felt close to anyone. Especially my PD. And certainly not to my physio with whom I was most intimate. (Think now, not a contradiction).

I began to do what I always did these days, vibrating my lips and spraying saliva all over. PD quickly stepped back from my bed. My parents stayed put. She slowly turned and took a small step towards them.

"I'm sorry it has come to this. But the good news is that we have the technology to replace any of his diseased genes or bad mutations with good ones. The latest accomplishments, embellishments really of the CRISPR-Cas9, now Cas20 will allow us to precisely remove the Huntingdon's gene."

"You mean, he will be rid of Huntingdon's, just like that?" asked my father, aware, as an historian that it is very difficult to change the past.

"Absolutely," smiled PD.

"And the side-effects?" asked mother.

"None that we know of," answered PT trying to be light-hearted, heartless bitch as she was. "Though most of the research has been conducted on the hairless guinea pig—*cavia porcellus*—that share ninety percent of genes with humans, or maybe it's the other way around." She smiled at her little joke, one that she repeated almost every day when talking to patients or potential patients.

My mother plucked up the courage to come to my bed and try to hold my hand. But it was impossible. I tried to hold it out, I really did because I felt sorry for her, but my fucking arm just kept flaying about, and almost knocked her head off.

Enough of this! I screamed something at PD. She stepped forward and gently pulled my mother away. "I think it's best to leave him be. I just wanted you to see him in his typical condition, so that after the precision surgery, you will see how good the cure is. And then her guilt overwhelmed her and she grabbed my mother in her arms and hugged her tightly.

"I'm so sorry you have to go through all this. I have always been against the de-gendering law enacted by the far left, or is it far right? Hard to tell these days."

I started to snort, making pig like noises. Seemed like I was doing it to get attention, but I wasn't. I simply had no control over what came out of my mouth, and where my body and its arms and legs would go next.

"So why have you really brought us here, the day before our de-gendering punishment?" asked my father belligerently.

PD looked guilty once more. "Because we need your parental approval to carry out the gene splicing on your son. He has been deemed unable to understand the procedures and unable to properly understand what is being asked of him."

"I don't know," said mother. "I don't think so.. Why don't you ask him yourself?"

PD hesitated. I tried to say something quietly and shake my head. All I could do was mumble, and screw up my face. This was surely a "No." My parents both edged forward to PD who looked at her, then down at me. They knew it.

"I think he is saying that he does not agree," muttered my mother timidly.

"Is that right?" asked PD leaning over my bed and speaking into my face our noses almost touching.

"Yeeehhhhairrr!" I growled.

It was clear. I had denied permission for them to splice my genome. But just to be sure they got it, I started to throw, what for me, was a tantrum, just to drive home my point. I thrashed and convulsed as hard as I could, let out the most horrible guttural and screaming noises, tried very hard to kick PD or anything else that was close.

My mother turned her head and I know she started to cry. She always did that when things got difficult. My father took her by the arm and with a sullen, silvery, unshaven face, stared at PD as if to say that it was she who had caused all the family's woes (he was right). He stared down at me with what was nothing less than a look of disgust. Then looked back at PD.

"As if it is not enough punishment for my wife and me to be de-gendered, we must look at this wretched mess of a child. And now, he refuses you permission to fix up the mess he has become. You are the doctor! Fix him!"

"Too bad I have not yet lost my hearing. Called me a child!

I'm thirty!" I cried to myself.

He turned and dragged my mother with him and when they reached the door a white coated attendant greeted them. "You need to come with me. The procedure takes only ten minutes for male, 15 minutes female.

PD looked on as I screamed and rolled off my bed, wriggling trying to get up on my hands and knees. I purposely slobbered on her white shoes.

"If you read the small print in the parental agreement form," called PD, "you would see that in the absence of approved parental consent, the attendant physician may make the necessary decision in the interests of the patient."

The door closed behind my parents. It was the last I would ever see them again, I thought. But how to communicate to my nemesis, or was she to be my savior?

PD produced a form from her clipboard and began to scribble something on it. With a massive effort I managed to reach up and bang the clipboard so that it flew out of her hand and clattered onto the polished floor. One thing I was still able to do was to move my eyes around and open or close my eyes, move my eyelids and frown. I managed to lie still for just a moment, then moved my eyes, wiggled my eyebrows. Now I had PT's attention. There was a book lying on the floor next to the pillow that was once on my bed. I managed to direct PT's attention to it. She picked up the book and opened it to a saliva soaked page where the paper had bubbled up. I gurgled or mumbled, trying not to yell. I raised my eyebrows and rolled my eyes. She looked closely at the page on which I had written some time ago when I was able to do fine motor movements.

The book was about autism, a collection of fascinating case studies highlighting the savants who gave autism a better name—well, appeared as talented freaks. Some had amazing memories (that was me—counting cards, remember?) others outstanding musical talents, born with perfect pitch, others incredible linguistic talents, could learn a new language in a few weeks. That's what I wanted. The case was high-lighted all the way through in bright yellow. I raised my eyebrows. Did PD understand me?"

PD herself frowned . And nodded slowly. I think I even managed a smile in response.

"You know that there is no single gene for autism. There's a number of genes involved. We don't really know which gene or genes, or which mutation switches on the particular excessive talents," she said, stooping over me, raising her voice as if I were deaf, which I wasn't (not yet anyway).

Then I discovered that I could also wrinkle my nose. And I could control my head well enough to lean over and plonk my nose on the yellow highlighted text. I screeched as loud as I could, "IIIIwwwaaaannntttttt," wrinkled my nose and snorted, and tried very hard to smile. Slobber and saliva and whatever else of slops that came out of my nose and mouth, ran all over the page, mixing with the yellow highlighter. This exertion was physically exhausting. I rolled over and off the bed and lay on my back my legs and arms flaying about like a beetle upended on its back.

PD looked down at me and grinned. She was obviously very pleased and I am sure she understood what I wanted. "OK. We will try to make your autism express itself as super language skills. And in exchange you will permit us to remove the Huntingtdon's gene. But remember, we do not know exactly whatever else removing the gene will do. In fact, it will be better if we instead of just removing it, we replace it with another gene, the one or more along with their mutations, that are related to super language skills."

I did my best to say yes, or express yes through my nose wrinkles.

"Deal?" she asked standing up straight, those buxom chest and shoulders once again as straight as any soldier at attention.

***

You may well ask. Why did I resist having my genes precisely edited to get rid of my Huntingdon's? Surely living a life as I was, was hardly living at all? There is some truth to that. But for the past seven or eight years a Huntingdon's patient is who I have been and I grew used to it. It was me, as horrible as it may have appeared. I liked my abominable self. And remember, I am—was—autistic from childhood. Other people were not especially who I wanted to be, or be with. I was always uncomfortable around them. It's why I liked my years in the MIT lab. I could spend my days engrossed in my experiments, my DNA mathematics. You see what I mean? It was not that big a step to become who I am now. Besides, as I conveyed to you, my daily animal needs were well looked after. I looked forward to my own personal physio servicing me, a therapy that I would immediately lose once I became "normal" again.

But even here, I have never been "normal." My life as a child and young adult, as they call us when we grow out of our teens was anything but that. I was autistic, remember. I was a savant. My memory was unbelievable. My math skills were incredible. I counted cards. I outsmarted the casinos. I worked hard in an MIT lab helping to develop CRISPR, the groundbreaking gene splicing technology. Yet when Huntingdon's arrived it was a kind of relief. What would it have been like spending my whole life as a freak mathematics wizard? Would I have ever found a mate, as obnoxious as was my *savant* self, absorbed totally in myself, unable to empathize to others. I could never see myself getting married (strange custom) and having children. Look what it did to my parents. I bet they regret it all, especially the boasting of my academic excellence. And it was my appearance on this planet that was in fact the death of them. Harassed by government regulators, despised by their neighbors, punished for thinking only of me and my welfare. Now to be de-gendered because they took a risk rather than allow the government regulators to play around with their genetic legacy, their genomes. It was a 50/50 chance I would be born with Huntingdon's—nobody knows the chances of being born an autistic savant. They gambled. They lost, at least in terms of the regulators they lost.

But I digress. It is enough to say that I will follow in their footsteps. I will gamble, a gambling man I am. Who knows how I will turn out? Huntingdon's will be gone for sure, the "me" I had grown used to, the me that was serviced by my physio.

I was going to say loving physio, but of course there was no love at all involved in our "relationship." I was serviced every other day, just like you get your car filled with gas, or your battery charged.

***

I had one last visit from my physio. And boy did I make it one to remember, not that I could, in my present autistic state, forget it. But who knows how I will turn out? PD arrived on time, accompanied by a string of attendants in white coats. Two regulators dressed in the current government style of dark blue tight Spandex-looking attire, the kind that elite swimmers used to wear when they competed, hung around the doorway. No one could figure out what they did. Technology had pretty much made them redundant. The quantum computers collected and stored all the information of everyone and everything. I suppose they reminded us of how things used to be.

"Well, young man," beamed PD. "Are you ready for your next trip?"

That seemed to be a most elegant way to characterize my situation. I grunted and splayed my arms and legs as usual. I already missed my physio. I grunted and tried not to display too much enthusiasm. After all, it was my life, really, my life, that was about to be edited.

"You know the routine," said PD as she inserted a cartridge into the vaccination gun. Why it was called that, I don't know. I wasn't being vaccinated against anything. No, I was being made into someone or something else.

You know how long it takes for a wound to heal? Well, that's how long it takes for the RNA molecules to invade every single one of the forty trillion cells of my body. When I awoke, I looked in awe at the precision doctors and lab assistants that crowded around. I was a thing of wonder. I had been a grand experiment. I blinked my eyes and turned my head this way and that. I slowly lifted both arms and put them down. Then I slowly drew up each leg then put them down.

"PD," I mumbled:

"I miei genitori stanno bene?

"Geht es meinen Eltern gut?

"我的父母还好吗？(Wǒ de fùmǔ hái hǎo ma?)

¿Mis padres están bien?

Мои родители в порядке?

Mes parents vont bien ?

Are my parents OK?"

Other Fiction By Colin Heston

Available from all bookstores around the world and digital platforms everywhere. **FREE on Read-Me.Org**

9/11 Two.

It's politics as usual when criminologist Maciver tries to thwart a terrorist drone tack on New York City Iranian terrorist Shalah Muhammad and his neurotic Russian American apprentice, Sarah Kohmsky, hire a Russian mafia boss, Uncle Sergey, and his evil nuclear scientist, Turgo, to hit Ground Zero on the anniversary of 9/11. Hearing of the plan from the CIA New York Mayor Ruth Newberg enlists Professor Larry Maciver, world renowned criminologist to thwart the attack. While the terrorists quietly orchestrate their attack, the drama unfolds as a battle between MacIver the careful scientist, and the impatient Buck Buick, Newark cop and former Marine bomb squad specialist. Will it be a drone, a missile, or a repeat of the 9/11 bombings? Das, Maciver's geeky assistant, thinks he has the answer. Can they save NYC or must it save itself?

The Tommie Felon Show
and Other Outrageous Stories.

A collection of stories ranging from the absurd to the improbable, with a cynical twist. These stories will keep you guessing, their deeper meaning will haunt you forever. "…engaging, hilarious, unique… a commentary on human desires, shortcomings and the society we live in…vivid and real…some of the stories jump out pf the pages." "Almost as sarcastic and cynical as Kurt Vonnegut, Colin Heston is an author to watch out for, now and in the future. —*Readers' Favorite*).

Miscarriages

Teen Chooka grows up in the weird world of 1950s Aussie pub life. When his alcoholic dad dies, he searches for his identity, and that of his shadowy underage girlfriend, Iris. Captivated by the pub's many crazy customers and their raucous stories, Chooka becomes a boozer just like them. But Iris, after a miscarriage, disappears and Chooka sets out on a search that takes him to foreign places including Melbourne university and Vietnam. The search ends in a Melbourne pub, where they start over, but this time there's a different ending. "…a brilliant, unforgettable book about real people…a sensitive, touching and poignant story." —*Reader's Favorite.*

Ferry to Williamstown

In this raucous Aussie story, corpses pop up in the Yarra river while Lizzie entertains her powerful and kinky clients in her Winnebago, parked on the ferry to Williamstown. Tightly bound Detective Striker, confronted by the mob of Catholics, wharfies and communists who rule Williamstown, struggles to solve the mystery. Lizzie gets engaged to her uncle Bobby, the lame ferry driver, and her mum, Babs, spellbound by the strange Father Zappia, tries to solve her own mystery of St. Robert's toe. She throws a raucous send-off party for Lizzie, and out of the chaos emerge many truths. "…a gritty but comedic family drama …with many threads to unravel, Ferry To Williamstown will reward those who can untie its hilarious Gordian knot." —*Reader's Favorite.*

MONA and Other Twisted Stories

The opening story of MONA, inspired by the Museum of Old and New Art located in Hobart, Tasmania, sets the stage for this collection of short stories that adds an Australian flavor to Colin Heston's acclaimed *The Tommie Felon Show.* The stories range across many styles, prose poems, jottings that are almost aphorisms, classic stories of human emotion and the contradictions of human existence, dystopian themes and settings, all engaging, never dull. "Many of the stories appear straightforward, but their simplicity brilliantly reveals many truths about modern society—so-called—and the impossibility of human ambitions reflected in the societies they have created… one has to look beyond the words and the events in these stories to really appreciate them." —*Reader's Favorite.*

Fault Lines

A series of 29 short stories inspired by the vicissitudes of punishment in all its forms, its deliverers and recipients. Its universality across cultures and at every level of social life from the kitchen to the battlefield never ceases to amaze. The stories unveil the diverse motives and excuses for punishment that paradoxically form the foundation of that great shibboleth of humanity: justice. The stories range through childhood spats to military encounters, , family discourse and dysfunction, to the puzzle of how criminal justice manages to match a punishment to its respective crime (it can't). Taken together, the stories ask one seemingly silly question of human history: which came first, the crime or the punishment?

About the Author

Colin Heston is the pen name of a criminologist of international repute. His previous fiction includes *9/11 Two* (2016), *The Tommie Felon Show* (2017), *Miscarriages* (2018, 2019 Australian edition), *Ferry to Williamstown* (2020), *MONA* collection of short stories (2021) and *Holy Water* (2022). Since 2021, he has published a new story every other Friday on the free library of open access publisher Read-Me.Org web site. In 2022 he also published a work of nonfiction, *The Art of Punishment,* in two volumes.